LADY *of* BREKEN MANOR

Interior design by Cora Johnson
Edited by Haley Swan and Lisa Shepherd
Cover design by Rachael Anderson
Cover image credit: Deposit Photos #60283083 and #3616042
Published by Mirror Press, LLC

ISBN-13: 978-1-947152-30-4

LADY *of* BREKEN MANOR

HEATHER B. MOORE

Mirror Press

LADY of BREKEN MANOR

No true lady can steal a loyal man from his fiancée, but what if that lady is a ghost?

Lady Charlotte is bored. So bored that when the owner of her manor in Scotland dies, she actually looks forward to haunting, uh, *meeting* the new owner. Too bad he's engaged. Because if he weren't, and if Charlotte could get him to fall in love with her, then the curse would finally be broken.

What curse, you ask? The curse that keeps Charlotte confined to an ancient manor decade after decade, playing parlor tricks on unsuspecting visitors. If only being a ghost weren't so tedious, Charlotte might actually enjoy her life-slash-death. But the new owner is making her rethink her entire existence.

CHAPTER 1

"THIS IS SOOO romantic," Michele said as she grabbed Sean's arm. "I mean, I can't believe you own a castle in Scotland!"

Sean jerked the wheel of the rented car to avoid a pothole. Michele squealed and only gripped Sean's arm tighter. It seemed that road maintenance was not high on the priority list for the small town of Melrose.

"It's not a *castle*," he corrected. "It's a manor, and I'm planning to sell the place. I just wanted to see it one time before I do."

Michele sighed one of her happy sighs. A sigh that used to make Sean smile, but lately, it had only annoyed him. Despite the fact that he and Michele had become engaged only the month before, he wished he hadn't brought her along. It was true she'd never traveled away from their home state of Colorado, but she'd been acting like a hyper kid in a chocolate factory since they first boarded the flight to New York City.

"You know the old-fashioned manors of England were really castles," Michele said in a dreamy voice. She redid the ponytail holder that held back her dark, curly hair. "Breken Manor . . . What a charming name. I'll bet there's a moat."

"There's no moat," Sean said. "And we're in Scotland, not England. I'm pretty sure there's a difference."

The information didn't seem to deter Michele's enthusiasm in the slightest.

"Oh my gosh, will you look at that?" she said in a shrieky voice, her brown eyes widening. "Cows!"

"There are cows in Colorado," he deadpanned.

"Not *Scottish* cows," she said with a giggle. She fell silent and looked at him. "You're acting so boring." Michele poked him in the ribs—his absolute least favorite habit of hers.

He'd once told her to stop, but that had only encouraged her to poke him more. She always did it when he was annoyed about something, so it only made him more ornery.

"What's wrong with you, Sean?" Michele asked, her thin brows pulling together. "Are you mad at me?"

It had been a really long twenty hours. Getting to the airport when Michele had been thirty minutes late, changing planes in New York after a delayed flight, listening to her incessant complaints about the airline food selections, finding out his suitcase hadn't quite made it on the international flight, and now, driving on the wrong side of the road with his fiancée who apparently wanted to know if he was mad at her.

"I'm just tired, babe," he said, hoping the endearment would mollify her. The last thing he needed was a nitpicky fight about how he was grumpy and how she thought he was mad at her for some unexplained reason. Couldn't he just be independently frustrated without having to overthink it or define their relationship?

Being engaged had one small advantage . . . Michele occupied herself more with wedding plans than with analyzing whether or not he was paying enough attention to her.

Damn . . . He really was grumpy. He loved Michele. Truly. They'd been friends since they were kids. Their families had always expected them to be together. They'd be getting married in a few months. They were on a mini vacation in Scotland. And he was being a jerk.

"Hey," he said, taking her hand and linking their fingers. "I think I just need a nap."

"Oh, I'm sure I can help with that," Michele said, another laugh following.

He hoped that she wouldn't be offended when he really *did* want to sleep. Their romantic life wasn't even close to what was portrayed in the movies. But the movies weren't real anyway, and Michele was a sweet person. She loved her family. She taught art and dance at the middle school. She was pouty when she didn't get her way, but overall, she had an upbeat personality.

They'd dated in high school. They'd dated in college. Michele was always there and had always been a part of his life. Like the sister he didn't have. No. *Not* like a sister. Because he was marrying her at the end of the summer. And he did have a sister: Eloise.

"There's the turnoff." Sean slowed the car and turned onto a narrow road. He had to stop whichever direction his thoughts were taking him. He didn't want to think about how he wasn't physically attracted to Michele. She was a woman, and she was pretty, but there wasn't that connection, or that "spark" he'd heard some of his business colleagues talk about. It was no use worrying about it now. Michele would be a great mom to their future kids, and their lives would continue on as they always had. Together.

The road Sean had turned on was in worse condition than the main road. He wondered if the shocks on the car would go out and if he'd have to pay for repairs when he turned in the rental car.

"Look at that old man," Michele commented. "Is he really pushing a cart? How provincial! Do you think he'd mind me taking his picture?"

The man was short and round, and he looked furious. Even from a distance, Sean could see the man was red-faced while he kicked one of the cart wheels. Sean slowed down and pulled alongside the man.

"Do you need help, sir?" Sean called out.

The man turned, as if shocked to see someone driving along the rutted lane.

"Got a new cart, lad?" he asked.

"No, but I can give you a ride . . . somewhere," Sean said, looking about and seeing only rolling hills. He turned off the ignition and climbed out. It felt good to stretch his cramped legs. "What happened?"

"The ole thing's lived its last days, I suppose." The

man squinted up at Sean. His round face seemed pleasant enough, when it wasn't reddened in anger.

Sean glanced inside the cart. It was filled with rocks. It was a wonder the man could push it at all. Suddenly curious, Sean asked, "Are you building something?"

"That wall beyond the field," he said. "The missus says it keeps me out of trouble."

Sean couldn't see any wall, so the man had a bit of a journey, it seemed. "Can I give you a ride somewhere?" he offered. There wouldn't be much room in the car for rocks, but maybe he could help out anyway.

Instead of answering Sean's question, the man said, "Aren't you a touch out of the way? I haven't seen the likes of you around here."

"I'm Sean McKinley," he said, "and this is my fiancée, Michele."

Michele was leaning on the car window sill and waved. "Hello."

"Nice to meet you both." The man stuck out his hand. "I'm Davis Farland. Where are you headed?"

"To the Breken castle," Michele piped up.

Farland narrowed his eyes. "The manor? What sort of business do you have there? It's been closed up for months."

"Sean inherited it," Michele said. "His sister Eloise is furious that he got it and not her. But he's going to sell the place. It's not like he can live in two places at once." She laughed.

Sean wished she'd been more delicate, or subtle, or something.

5

Farland didn't smile. In fact, he took a step back as if he'd been startled. "You're *that* McKinley?"

Sean didn't know exactly how common the McKinley name was, but he said, "Yes, sir."

"And you're wantin' to *sell* the place?" Farland asked, as if it were somehow an insult.

Sean hesitated. He didn't know if this Farland man should know all of his business. But perhaps it would lead to a buyer. The lawyer who'd gone over the details of his great-uncle's will had told him that the manor had been renovated over the decades, but not much had been done for the past five years. When Sean's great-uncle died last month, the manor had come to Sean. His Great-Uncle McKinley had been the eccentric sort, too rich for his own good, and when he'd purchased the manor in Scotland about ten years ago and decided to live in it, everyone in Sean's extended family had thought Uncle McKinley had truly lost his mind.

But Sean didn't want to judge the man without seeing the place first. Especially since it now belonged to him. "My fiancée is right. We don't have use for the manor, no matter how charming it might be. We're here to visit the place and look it over. Perhaps see if any repairs need to be made before we put it on the market."

"He's in construction back in Colorado—you know, the United States of America," Michele overexplained. "He'll probably want to renovate the whole thing before he sells it."

"We're only here for a week," he reminded her and turned back to Farland. "Is it in decent repair?"

6

Farland scoffed as if Sean had said something completely ridiculous.

"Yes, it's in good repair," Farland conceded. "But you won't be selling the place."

"Why not?" both Sean and Michele asked at the same time.

Farland looked behind him as if he expected someone to be standing there. Then he lowered his voice. "Because the lady won't allow it."

Sean stared at the man, wondering what he could possibly mean. "*Lady?*"

Farland looked behind him again, then took a step closer as if he was worried someone on this deserted road might overhear him. "Lady Charlotte's known for running out potential buyers if she doesn't like them. You, on the other hand, don't have much of a choice because you inherited it. Luckily, she had a soft spot for Ole McKinley."

"Who's Charlotte?" Michele asked.

It was Sean's exact question as well.

"Shhh," Farland said, raising a hand. "She must be addressed as *Lady,* and only in the most reverent tones. She's royalty, you know, and she's got a temper, that one."

Sean exchanged glances with Michele. He'd never heard of this Charlotte person. Wouldn't the lawyer have told him when they went over the inheritance paperwork? "From documents that I received, it seems that the manor belongs to me, and I can do with it as I will."

Farland chuckled and placed a hand on Sean's shoulder. "Best of luck to you then, lad." He turned away, shaking his head. He proceeded to heft a few of the rocks into his arms and continue walking up the road, leaving the cart behind. As Farland walked away, Sean realized that something like a warning had knotted in his stomach. But a warning about what?

"What a strange man," Michele said. "Must be one of those superstitious sorts."

Sean couldn't agree more. Just then a cool breeze stirred around him, defying the afternoon heat, and swept across his neck like icy fingers trailing his skin.

CHAPTER 2

LADY CHARLOTTE OF Breken Manor knew they were coming long before they actually appeared in the lane leading up to her home. It didn't take much sense to know that once Old McKinley died, the manor would go to someone else—a distant relative, no doubt, since Old McKinley had no children of his own. And within weeks or months, that distant someone would show up. Ogle the place, kick a few baseboards, then make an accounting list of repairs in order to turn a tidy profit by selling the place . . . again. Nothing new, really.

She watched the modern contraption called a car turn at the end of the lane and begin its bumpy trek toward the house. From her attic perch, the rolling hills surrounding the manor were green and lush in the early summer afternoon. It was Charlotte's favorite time of year, with the land warming up and the unending scent of wildflowers and budding roses in the air.

Her roses were just starting their first round of blooms, so she'd spent most of the day in the gardens, since Old McKinley was no longer around to do her bidding.

Charlotte released a melancholy sigh. She would miss Old McKinley. He'd been a good sort, if not stubborn. They'd had their arguments, but at least he'd agreed not to sell the manor during his lifetime. Not when they got along so well. The last thing Charlotte wanted to do was train a new owner. If McKinley had tried to sell the place, Charlotte would have driven away every potential buyer. She'd warned him more than once.

The car below stopped in the driveway, and the doors opened simultaneously. Charlotte watched with curiosity as two people emerged from the car. The first thing that struck her was their ages. They were young, perhaps in their twenties. Not much older than Charlotte herself—or how old she'd been upon her death in 1860.

The woman tilted her head up and scanned the front of the manor, her red-lipsticked mouth forming an O. She waved to the man who'd also climbed out of the car, and then she pointed frantically at something, as if she were a child at a circus.

Charlotte immediately disliked the woman. But that wasn't unusual. She never liked the women who came to live at Breken. And at the same time, she always developed a soft spot in her heart for the men. Not all the men, of course, but most of them. This was quite ironic since it was because of a man that Charlotte couldn't pass to the other side.

The King of England's brother, to be exact. Of course, he was long dead now, but that hadn't stopped the curse uttered by Charlotte's mother ages ago on their mutual death beds.

If it hadn't already been nearly two hundred years since her mother's death, Charlotte might feel melancholy, but time truly did heal all wounds. It just didn't heal curses. Apparently, those had to be "fulfilled."

"Sean," the woman said, her voice the high-pitched feminine type.

Charlotte didn't need to open the attic window to hear the couple below. Her hearing was quite amplified—one of the advantages of the dead.

The man named Sean didn't answer the woman. Instead, he seemed to be making a phone call on one of those cellular devices. Relocating the cellular devices of visitors at the manor was one of Charlotte's favorite things to do. She always found a great deal of amusement watching the visitor run about the house, eyes wide, chest heaving in panic, breathing erratic, as they looked for their phones. Charlotte never put it under a cushion or behind a vase . . . No, that would be too cruel. She'd simply put it in another room. Preferably Old McKinley's.

He used to rant at her for that one.

Sean still hadn't looked up, much to the woman's chagrin. Instead, he was waving his hand as he spoke on his phone. Did he think he was leading an orchestra in the middle of the manor driveway? Charlotte smiled and rested her chin on her hand as she continued to watch. If nothing else, the next few hours would be entertaining.

She often placed bets with herself. How fast could she send someone running out of the house? Her only rule was that she couldn't actually appear to anyone. Not that anyone but those whom she allowed could see her anyway. Unless she was caught off guard. Which meant that the man with the brown hair speaking on his cell phone would probably be able to see her if he looked up to where that increasingly annoying woman was pointing. The presence of this man had somehow caught her off guard.

Things were about to change, Charlotte thought glumly. Her break from the museum visitors was now over. Visitors came to the manor to tour the museum rooms. The manor wasn't exactly a museum registered with the county or anything, but Old McKinley had preserved the late Victorian style furniture, stuffed it all into a couple of rooms on the main level, then charged visitors to tour those rooms. It was quite brilliant, really, and in truth, those rooms were Charlotte's favorites in the entire house. Well, except for her cozy attic room, which she kept locked at all times. She didn't need a door, but it helped to keep everyone else out.

"Are they bringing out your suitcase?" the woman's voice cut into Charlotte's reminiscing.

Charlotte's gaze snapped back to the window.

"It will be delivered tomorrow," the man said, his tone sounding dejected. And then he looked up.

Blast. Charlotte hurried to hide behind the curtains. If this McKinley was as astute as his uncle, he might sense her presence, and it would ruin all the fun. But he wasn't looking at the attic window where she'd just been standing. He was looking at the different levels of the roofs. And his eyes were a deep green. His jaw square and sturdy. His brows were drawn together in concentration, or was it puzzlement? Or perhaps irritation? *With the woman?* That would be quite lovely, Charlotte decided. Nothing was more fun than pitting two lovers against each other.

Sean lifted a hand and did some of his own pointing. Charlotte had already noticed that his shoulders were broad and his forearms tanned and muscled like a farmer's, although she doubted very much he was a farmer. It was quite out of fashion these days. People bought their food at grocery stores.

"The second roof looks about ready to collapse," Sean said.

Charlotte straightened with indignation. What was he talking about? The roofs of Breken Manor were perfectly maintained. She'd made sure of it—reminding Old McKinley of what needed to be done. It wouldn't speak well about her if the manor she'd been eternally condemned to live in decided to go and fall apart around her.

But there had been some rather heavy rains as of late, and Old McKinley had let a few things slide the past year or two. Perhaps it had been three or four years. It was blasted difficult to track time when you were dead. Especially after the first one hundred years.

"Let's go inside," the woman said.

"I'm going to walk around it first," Sean replied.

Good for him, decided Charlotte. He wasn't letting his wife or girlfriend tell him what to do. Not that Charlotte herself was any sort of demure female. She'd cheered on all feminist advances over the centuries, but she also didn't like to see a pistol-whipped man.

"Be careful in there, Michele," Sean called to the woman as the front door rattled below.

Michele. So that was her name.

Charlotte moved out of the attic room, not bothering with any door, of course. She simply walked through the wall. She could have floated, or heaven forbid, even flown. But ladies never floated or flew—that was for those scurrilous witch types. She walked like the good-mannered and well-bred lady that she was.

She walked down the stairs, only skipping a couple of them, to the second floor. She hurried, although still keeping it to a ladylike walk, to the Blue Room. The high windows gave her an excellent view of the back gardens.

And there he was, slowly walking around the house. Sean held a notepad in his hand and was writing down things as he looked over the patio flagstones and the railing. The sun's orange-yellow afternoon rays filtered through the tall trees that lined the patio. With that sort of back lighting, Charlotte couldn't help but notice the way Sean's button-down shirt tapered at his narrow waist and how his denim pants seemed well worn, yet nicely formed over what she guessed to be muscular thighs. If this man had lived during the Victorian era, what a sight he would have been in fitted breeches.

Charlotte! Her mother's voice echoed in her head. It was quite bothersome when that happened. Sometimes Charlotte wondered if her mother hadn't truly crossed to the other side, but had remained at the manor as well. Whenever Charlotte had an untoward thought, well, *toward* a man, her mother's voice promptly started

14

reprimanding her. And reminding her of that infernal curse.

Charlotte spun around, scanning the very empty Blue Room. "Mother, I don't know if you're here or not, but might you please stop shouting at me? It's quite disconcerting."

The curse (as uttered by Charlotte's mother, Constance) echoed through her mind: *Upon my death and the death of my illegitimate daughter Charlotte, in retribution for all the wrongs that have been done to us, in treating us like we were second-class and banishing us to this unholy corner of Scotland, the Manor of Breken will be haunted by my daughter Charlotte until the owner of the manor demonstrates pure and true love for her. Only the power of that previously stated love has the power to atone for all that has befallen us.*

The curse was quite lengthy, Charlotte admitted, but what she didn't understand was why *she'd* been sentenced to the haunting. Charlotte hadn't been wronged, at least not as much as her mother had. In fact, Charlotte had been quite pleased with life at the manor. They had servants and an excellent cook, and the stable master was a fine man to gaze upon each morning during her riding lessons.

Life hadn't been all bad.

Charlotte continued speaking aloud to her mother. "And, besides, if I can't admire a man, then how am I supposed to get one interested in me enough to fall in love and break this blasted curse?"

Her mother had hated it when Charlotte had used the word "blast," or "blasted," or any derivative thereof.

No one responded, and this pleased Charlotte. It seemed she'd just found a way to stop her mother's intrusions. Not that she was completely betting on it. And not that she was a gambler in the first place. At least with money.

Feeling a bit triumphant nonetheless, Charlotte turned back to the window. Too bad Old McKinley had been in love with his wife—even though she'd passed on— and couldn't ever quite look upon Charlotte with that type of affection. It now appeared that Sean had left the patio in front of the gardens and had started to walk to the far end of the house. Charlotte craned against the window, tracking his progress. But the window was proving much too restrictive, so she simply poked her head through the glass.

Sean had stopped and was looking, *again*, up at the roof. What was this man's obsession with roofs? At least this new profile view gave her something more to admire . . . such as *his* profile. Even though she hadn't exactly stood right in front of him, she could tell he was taller than she, and this was quite a feat.

In the Victorian era, men had been rather shorter than they now seemed to be in the twenty-first century. American men were particularly tall, and Sean was most definitely American. Charlotte wondered what it would be like to stand in front of Sean and look up into his eyes as he gazed down at her.

"You're being ridiculous." That was definitely not her mother's voice.

It was Michele's.

The woman's footsteps traipsed up the stairs to the

second floor, and so Charlotte turned to watch the woman enter the Blue Room, talking to herself.

If the one-sided conversation hadn't been so disparaging to Charlotte, she might have laughed about it.

"There's no *Lady Charlotte* here," muttered Michele, snooping through the drawers of the solid oak credenza. "This place is as musty as a tomb." The woman swiped a long finger over the credenza and came away with a coating of dust. She sneezed.

"No *lady* would let this place go to rot," Michele said, sneezing again. "I can barely breathe in this place for all the dust. And the heat . . . it's unbearable! Hasn't anyone heard of a fan?" She turned and walked out of the room.

Hmm, Charlotte thought. *I have something in common with Michele. We both talk to ourselves. A lot.*

"Sean," Michele called out, and Charlotte winced at the squealing pitch of her voice.

Charlotte followed Michele along the hallway and watched her walk down the stairs to the main level. Michele opened the back door, and Sean walked into the house.

"Wow," he said, looking around. "This woodwork is amazing." He crossed to the wall of the foyer and examined the carved paneling.

Charlotte smiled, pleased that he appreciated the details of the house she'd taken care of. Well, it was Old McKinley's upkeep work, guided by her advice.

"It's really dark, though," Michele complained. "We should paint it white, or maybe that trendy light gray."

Sean looked up at Michele, and the shocked

expression on his face mirrored the sudden palpitations of Charlotte's heart. Well, her former heart.

"We're not touching the paneling," Sean said. He ran a hand over the wood, and for a moment Charlotte wondered what it might be like to have that same hand running over her arm.

The temperature in the room did seem a bit too warm, now that she thought about it. A fan wasn't such a bad idea after all.

Michele moved off into the kitchen, and Charlotte heard a couple of things being banged around. The woman had better not be touching the heirloom china. But instead of checking up on Michele, Charlotte continued to watch Sean.

She enjoyed how he noticed small details, appreciated them, then wrote things into his notebook. She stepped closer. Not close enough to touch, of course, but close enough to smell him. That was one thing she missed about being alive. She couldn't wear perfume or benefit from scented bathing. In fact, if she smelled of anything, it would be of her garden roses. At least, Old McKinley had often remarked that he knew when she was in the room because he could smell roses.

But Sean didn't seem to notice anything about her— not her scent, not her hovering breath, not her closeness.

She gave the tiniest of sighs and started to read his writing.

Oh no. He was making lists. Lists of things to repair.

Charlotte's face grew hot, spreading to her neck and chest and arms, and ... the notebook thumped to the floor.

Sean didn't move for a moment. Neither did Charlotte. She hadn't meant to knock it out of his hands quite so suddenly. She could have waited until these mortals were sleeping and then conveniently taken it outside and rubbed a little dew onto the pages. Instead, she had to go and practically rip it out of his hands and throw it onto the hardwood floor, as if she were a child of three fighting over a toy.

Her eyes were stinging with shame, and she turned away from Sean, wanting to move away quickly.

She stopped, though, at the base of the stairs and looked back at him over her shoulder.

He was still staring down at the notebook, a crease between his brows, as if he were trying to solve a great mathematical formula.

And then, before she could glide up the stairs, he lifted his head and looked right at her.

Charlotte couldn't move. She knew he couldn't see her, but why was his gaze so directly fastened on hers? The sun had finally settled onto the horizon, casting its deep orange and gold rays through the windows of the house. Sean's hair looked positively golden, and Charlotte realized she hadn't noticed before how his hair had a slight wave to it.

He looked so healthy, and strong, and ... alive. That's what had her disconcerted, she decided. He was so alive, and she was *so* not.

Then Sean took a step forward, and Charlotte stopped breathing—well, she would have if she could actually breathe. She stopped anyway because this very handsome man, this very tall man, with broad shoulders, a penetrating gaze, and hands that looked capable enough to build an entire castle, was walking toward her.

Charlotte gazed into his eyes, wanting them to see her, to truly see her. Although he was looking at her, she knew he couldn't. She barely moved aside as he took that final step to the base of the stairs. She turned to look at the painting on the wall that he'd become entranced with.

She felt fluttery and light as Sean studied the art.

The woman in the painting was someone that Charlotte barely knew anymore. It was a painting of herself at the age of twenty, commissioned and completed only a few months before her death. It was the last likeness that had ever been done of her in life.

Charlotte almost wished she still had that white satin gown with the blue trim along the bodice and French lace at the sleeves. Alas, the dress was carted off to a museum long ago when the owner before McKinley took it upon himself to eke out every spare coin from the manor.

Charlotte's hair had been piled into a lovely stack of ringlets for the sitting. The honey-gold strawberry locks had been much commented on during social events. Red hair was common in this county, but Charlotte was part German, and with her heritage came blue eyes and a softer strawberry coloring.

"Lady Charlotte," Sean said.

Her mouth fell open, until she realized he was reading the artist's caption on the corner of the painting.

"Eighteen sixty," Sean continued. "Remarkable."

Charlotte liked the way he said "remarkable." It sounded like a term of endearment.

CHAPTER 3

SEAN GAZED AT the painting at the base of the stairs. The woman in the painting was Charlotte—Lady Charlotte. So this was who Farland had been talking about. But this painting was completed in 1860. Which meant the young woman had been dead for many years.

Although the proportions of the hands and shoulders seemed slightly off, the woman in the painting was beautiful. Her honey-red hair was pulled away from her face into an elaborate updo, with wispy ringlets on each side. And the white dress she wore offset her cream-colored skin well. Perhaps it was the afternoon light filling the foyer, but the woman's eyes seemed to glitter blue. Well, maybe not exactly *glitter*, but her eyes were an unusual blue, both dark and light at the same time. He wondered how accurate the artist had been at capturing the woman's likeness.

Her expression seemed both haughty and amused at the same time, almost as if she had some Madonna-type secret. Or perhaps she was amused by the artist. The glow of the afternoon sun's rays spilling across the painting must have been creating some sort of illusion, because for a second, Sean thought he saw the woman in the painting take a breath. Impossible, he knew. Yet, the very next instant, he could have sworn that something breezed past his arm.

He turned around, his heart in his throat. No one was there. Michele was making quite a racket in the kitchen, calling out random bits of information. Whatever Farland had been referring to when he spoke of Lady Charlotte must have somehow worked its way into Sean's psyche, and now, he was imagining things. Paintings didn't breathe. And unseen objects didn't float around, brushing his arm.

He turned back to the painting, compelled to look at the woman again. She was young, perhaps in her early twenties. What had her life been like? He couldn't stop staring into the woman's blue eyes, which should have been strange in itself, but doubly strange because the next thing he knew, he was asking his questions aloud, as if he could have a conversation with a painting. "What did you love, Lady Charlotte? What did you despise? Did you walk these very stairs? Did you watch the sun set each evening?"

Of course there was no answer from the woman in the painting, but oddly enough, Sean sensed that she might be listening. Ridiculous, he knew. He noticed the gilt-edged frame seemed to be discolored. He ran a finger along the frame and wondered if there was a solution that might clean it up. Rubbing alcohol would be too strong. Perhaps something like a jewelry cleaner.

"I prefer the sunrise," Michele whispered behind him.

Sean smiled and turned, but Michele wasn't there.

The hairs on his neck rose, and his heart thumped out of rhythm. "Michele?" he called.

"Yeah?" she hollered from the kitchen.

She hadn't sneaked into the foyer and whispered against his neck.

Now, he was hearing things. *I prefer the sunrise,* the imaginary voice had said.

Farland's words came to mind: "She's royalty, you know, and she's got a temper, that one."

Sean looked again at the woman in the painting. Perhaps the glint in her eyes wasn't amusement, but something more temperamental. Maybe she hadn't wanted her portrait painted.

He decided to try something, although if anyone knew about it, they'd think he was out of his mind.

"Why do you prefer the sunrise?" he asked the woman in the painting.

The air felt still around him. Michele was humming something in the kitchen, or maybe it was muttering. Sean kept his full gaze and attention locked on the painting.

And the whispered voice returned. Soft, caressing, and moving about Sean as if it were just out of his hearing range.

"When the sun sets, it means I've been trapped another day," the voice whispered. "When the sun rises, hope grows again that I might yet cross to the other side."

Sean didn't move. He didn't turn around. No one would be there. Someone had heard him and replied, and it wasn't Michele. That left only one possibility. His jet lag had just taken his exhaustion to a whole new level.

"What are you doing?" Michele asked, her very much non-whispering voice rang out. "I've called you three times. I can't reach the coffee pot. Someone put it on top of the cupboard."

Sean blinked and slowly turned, feeling as if he'd just awakened from a deep sleep. Michele stood before him, her hand perched on her hip and her eyes narrowed. Her expression annoyed.

"Sorry," Sean said, although he wasn't sure why Michele wanted coffee in the late afternoon when they were both dead tired and hadn't slept for nearly twenty-four hours. "I'll come get it."

"Why's your notebook on the floor?" Michele continued.

Sean had no answer, but Michele would never stop with just one question.

"I was just checking out some things." He moved past her and walked into the kitchen. It took him only a moment to find the coffee pot, and he brought it down onto the counter. It was a newer model, which also made him wonder why it had been stashed on top of the cupboard. Surely his great-uncle had used it.

He plugged it into the outlet on the wall above the counter. A green light lit up. "Seems to be working at least," he called to Michele. Where had she gone now? "Do you want—"

Michele screeched, and Sean froze.

His first thought was . . . Well, he wasn't going to let himself complete that first thought. There were probably mice in the house considering how long it had been empty. But as he hurried to the foyer, he stopped cold. Michele was backed up against the wall, her trembling hand pointing to the painting at the bottom of the stairs.

"She blinked," Michele whispered in a horrified voice.

"What?" Sean said, because he was too stupefied to say anything else. "That's not possible—"

"She blinked!" Michele screamed, and then she threw herself at Sean.

He nearly stumbled backward as he caught the hysterical Michele. "Come on, let's sit down in the kitchen."

Michele was shaking and crying and talking faster than Sean could possibly understand. He'd never seen her completely fall apart like this. Somehow, he got her to sit down, and he sat next to her, keeping his arm around her.

"You're exhausted," Sean said. "I don't care that it's not dark yet, we should go to bed."

Michele mumbled something while nodding.

"Come on then," Sean said, standing up and pulling her to her feet.

He led her into the bedroom where she'd unpacked a few of her things, and he tucked her beneath the blanket, then drew the curtains across the window.

"Stay with me," Michele said, reaching for Sean's arm.

He kicked off his shoes and climbed onto the bed next to her. She fell asleep within moments, but it took quite a bit longer for Sean to follow suit.

CHAPTER 4

CHARLOTTE PACED OUTSIDE the bedroom that Sean had led Michele into. She'd heard their murmured voices, and then silence. Had they fallen asleep already? She supposed she should feel the tiniest bit remorseful about scaring Michele, but it was mostly an experiment to see how perceptive the woman was. It turned out that Michele was very, very perceptive.

Charlotte paused in her pacing, wondering exactly what was going on in that bedroom. They were no longer talking. Even though she was a ghost, she did have some manners. She never walked through shut doors, especially into bedrooms. She didn't always stick to her rules, but she tried harder with this one over the others.

When she was quite sure they must both be asleep, she decided she'd peek in on them. She didn't pretend to be a hostess in any way, but it couldn't hurt to make sure the new owner and his wife/girlfriend were comfortable in the bed.

Another owner who had his heart spoken for. Why

couldn't the next owner be a single, available man? One that would fall madly and truly in love with her? Charlotte wrinkled her nose as she passed through the door and spied the couple asleep on the bed. Michele was underneath the covers, her snoring very light and ladylike.

Sean had an arm propped behind his head, his eyelids shut, his breathing even. The scene was peaceful and shouldn't have made Charlotte feel envious, but it did. She'd been young when she'd died and hadn't experienced the love of a man. She hadn't experienced marriage, or known what it was like to sleep next to someone she loved.

It seemed the living didn't know how much they truly had. How the things they took for granted were impossibilities to Charlotte.

She leaned against the wall and watched the sleeping couple as she wondered how many decades, or centuries, more she'd have to watch other people live their lives. Charlotte realized the room had grown violet with twilight, and she'd dallied much too long in the bedroom.

She didn't like to wander about the house or around the estate after dark. It made her feel even more isolated from life because everyone lay asleep while she couldn't rest. So as soon as the sun set, she'd make her way to the attic room where she'd wait until the sun rose. Mostly she just watched the horizon, although sometimes she read.

Reading was a favorite pastime of hers, but there were only so many times one could read the same books over and over.

Charlotte ignored the attic's haphazardly stacked bookcases tonight and walked to the window. The moon hung low in the sky as the stars glittered across the wide expanse. It was on nights like these, where the moon seemed to light the entire countryside, that Charlotte missed her childhood the most.

Her governess, Miss Lucille, had been stern but kind, and they'd invented a dozen ways to fall asleep. One of them was to count the stars, another was to whisper wishes to the moon, a third way was to keep her eyes closed and imagine that she was floating above the trees on a soft cloud. As a child, Charlotte had trouble falling asleep because she always felt there was so much to learn and so many things to do.

Charlotte still had trouble falling asleep. In fact, she hadn't fully slept in over 150 years. She sometimes thought she'd nodded off, but then wasn't entirely sure because she never seemed to miss a moment in time.

Perhaps she should try counting stars again. Charlotte lay down on her bed, which was situated across from the window so that she had a clear view of the night sky. She never counted minutes during the night, although she was fully aware of the time passing. It was possibly two or three hours later when she heard footsteps coming up the stairs. She sat up and held her breath—an unnecessary habit—and listened.

Yes, someone was definitely on the stairs.

Charlotte slipped off the bed.

She moved across the room and walked through the wall to the corner of the outer hallway where she'd have the first view of whoever was coming. The hallway was dark, of course, but the person had some sort of flashlight. A phone light, to be exact.

Sean's head and broad shoulders came into view, and then he was standing at the top of the stairs, sweeping his phone light across the wall until he saw the light switch.

Charlotte hadn't been entirely happy when the house had been outfitted with electricity, until she figured out that turning on lights in the dark rooms of unsuspecting guests was quite entertaining. But for Sean to be here now, turning on a light, told Charlotte that he was no fool.

He was on a hunt for answers.

Light flooded the upper hallway, chasing away every bit of darkness. But still Charlotte was completely invisible to the living eye.

Sean looked about. His hair was mussed, and Charlotte had the uncanny urge to cross to him and smooth it away from his forehead. In one hand he held his phone, in the other, a thin book of some sort. He did look tired. He'd only slept two or three hours by Charlotte's estimation. But even through his exhaustion, she sensed his intelligence, his steadiness, his curiosity.

It all made her want to sigh. The problem was, sometimes her sighs were audible, since they took so much effort to produce. So she refrained.

Sean cleared his throat, then gave a little cough. "I can't believe I'm doing this," he said.

Charlotte straightened from where she was leaning against the wall. Who was he speaking to?

He cleared his throat again.

Perhaps he was coming down with a cold? It would be miserable to listen to him coughing, sniffling, and blowing his nose during his stay. Not exactly a romantic sentiment. Of course, Charlotte didn't have romantic designs on this man. She'd just have to wait until the next man came along.

"Hello?" Sean said.

Charlotte drew her eyebrows together. *Hello?* Who was he speaking to?

"Miss, uh, Lady Charlotte?" he said, a bit louder this time.

Charlotte stifled a gasp. He *was* speaking to her. He ... he ... Charlotte turned and stepped through the closed door behind her, landing her in the closet of her attic bedroom. Why an attic ever needed a closet, she didn't know. An attic was supposed to be its own, very large closet.

But Charlotte needed a moment. Sean was looking for her, *speaking* to her, which meant that he believed she existed.

"Lady Charlotte," he began again, his voice trembling slightly as if he were nervous ... or scared? "I'm not sure how to do this—how to find you—but I figured you'd be up here somewhere. I mean, spirits float when they don't have a body, right? So I thought you'd be in the highest part of the house."

Makes sense, Charlotte thought. She liked that about Sean. He was logical.

The knob of the attic door rattled. "Oh, it's locked," Sean muttered, his tone filled with disbelief. He tried it again, and Charlotte gritted her teeth together. She didn't have many pet peeves, but rattling was one of them. She had never been a ghost that rattled things. It all seemed so archaic.

And then, to her horror, he knocked. "Lady Charlotte?" he said through the door.

Did he not care about waking that Michele woman downstairs? It was one thing to have a handsome man believe in her and pursue her, but if Michele joined him, Charlotte knew she'd lose what little temper she was clinging to right now and give them both the fright of their lives.

One of her more glorious frights had been moving an entire rug from beneath the patron's feet. Another time, she'd taken all of the books off the library shelves, setting them in neat piles about the room. Her favorite, which she did quite often, was putting bed pillows under the beds. No one wanted a dusty pillow—and of course they had to find said pillow first.

She'd made the painting blink before, and really, it was only a trick of the light. But not everyone caught it, so it wasn't her favorite prank. Once she'd blown on a woman's cheek as she walked down the stairs. As luck, or *bad* luck, would have it, the woman lost her balance and ended up falling and breaking her wrist. This only created more misery, since the woman in question was laid up at the manor for an entire week longer than planned.

"Lady Charlotte?" Sean called again as he knocked.

"Fine," Charlotte muttered to herself. She moved out of the closet and opened the door to the attic. Sean stood in the hallway, his expression stunned as the door suddenly opened before him. She hoped he wasn't about to faint.

That was so nineteenth century.

Sean recovered quickly, and some of the color came

back into his face. He switched on his phone light again and made a wide sweeping arc of the room.

Charlotte turned to see what he was looking at. Seeing it through his eyes made her realize that the place needed to be tidied up a bit. Her books were stacked every which way in the double bookcase. Her vanity table was filled with dusty perfume bottles and trinket jewelry boxes. She had an entire collection of hat boxes stacked in the far corner, and the boxes were leaning precariously to one side. There were three rocking chairs. She didn't sit in them and rock, per se, but she had an affinity for good craftsmanship, so she'd locked them away in the attic so that none of the greedy manor owners could sell them.

Sean spotted the light switch and flipped it.

Charlotte smiled to herself. She'd unscrewed the light bulb ages ago so that the curious who chose to venture into the attic room on rare occasions were discouraged.

Apparently she'd underestimated Sean. He stepped into the room, completely undeterred, and crossed to the window. Pulling the drapes wide let the moonlight spill into the attic and, in conjunction with the light from the hallway, gave Sean plenty of light to check out his surroundings. Interestingly enough, he crossed to the bed. The bedspread wasn't all that dusty, although the fabric was a now-dingy white eyelet.

Sean stared down at the bed for a moment, completely silent. What was he thinking about? Charlotte wished that reading minds was in her repertoire of ghostly talents, but alas, it was not.

"Is this where you sleep?" Sean said into the absolute quiet.

It was strange having him speak to her, in her bedroom, as far as strange things went.

Sean released a sigh. "*Do* you sleep, Lady Charlotte? Or do you roam the rose gardens at night?"

"I do not roam, *ever*," Charlotte said before she could stop herself.

Sean whirled around.

He'd *heard* her.

She stepped back because she realized how close she'd been standing to him.

He was staring at her—or more accurately, *through* her. His eyes were wide in the dimness, but he didn't go pale like he had when she'd answered the door.

"You *are* here," he said, triumph in his voice. "I *knew* it!"

Charlotte folded her arms. She hadn't even shown herself to this man; he seemed to have a bit too much confidence for her taste.

"So," he continued, stepping right toward her as if he could see her. His gaze was moving from one side of the room to another, searching for any sign of her. Well, he wouldn't get it. "Are you truly Lady Charlotte? Like Davis Farland said? Or are you someone else?"

How impertinent of him. "Of course I'm Lady Charlotte," she said. "How many ghosts do you think are at Breken Manor?"

He chuckled. *Chuckled!* "I don't know the laws of the spirit world. My apologies."

Well, an apology was definitely progress. But he

could use some correcting. "I'm not in the spirit world, obviously," she replied. "I'm stuck at Breken Manor as you have deduced."

Sean nodded, still looking around as if desperate to find a place for his gaze to land. "I'm sorry about that. Has it been so awful?"

What a strange question. Of course it was awful. Well, not *entirely* awful. Right now, it was quite interesting. No one had told her they were sorry for her plight. It made her feel ... warm and comforted somehow. It also made her feel more miserable. She really did want to move on and not be stuck in this limbo of life—or death.

"I have born it well, I think," Charlotte said, although she heard the doubt in her own voice.

He was smiling. Back to impertinence, it seemed. "I've heard otherwise," he said.

Charlotte stared at him, hard. And for a moment, she wished he could see her. She'd definitely give him the evil eye so that he'd regret his words. "Explain yourself," she demanded.

CHAPTER 5

SEAN COULDN'T BELIEVE he was talking to a disembodied voice. A ghost, a spirit, an apparition—an *invisible* apparition. But it was the same voice he'd heard that afternoon when he'd been talking to the painting. He had a feeling if he started asking questions, she wouldn't be able to resist answering them.

He'd slept for a couple of hours, and then something had awakened him with a start. He'd chalked it up to sleeping in an unfamiliar house with different sounds. But then his mind wouldn't shut off, and he was hyper-focusing on Michele's light snoring. Other thoughts started to race through his mind about how she'd claimed to see the painting of Lady Charlotte blink. Impossible, he knew. But he'd also had some strange things happen to him. Exhaustion had played a few tricks. So he finally climbed out of bed and went to the kitchen.

He rummaged some stale biscuits, bit into one, then walked into the library. His uncle had a decent-size desk made of lustrous cherry wood. Sean switched on the desk lamp and settled into the smooth leather chair. It creaked a bit when he sat down. Sean opened the top drawer of the desk and found a financial ledger. When he scanned the dates, he saw it was about twenty years old. None of it would be of much use now.

Another thin book was inside the same drawer, and he pulled it out. Opening to the middle, he realized it was a diary of sorts. Sean flipped to the front. The opening date was two years ago, and the author? His great-uncle.

Sean thought he'd be reading about the slow but sometimes eccentric life of a widower who'd sold everything in the States to buy a manor in Scotland. But, no. The diary was not about plodding around the village, investigating local ruins, or random life philosophies. It was a diary of Uncle McKinley's interactions with Lady Charlotte. Who happened to be a ghost.

Entry 1:

Dear Diary,

It's quite a cliché to write "Dear Diary," I know. But I cannot exactly talk to others about the truth of my life here at Breken Manor. There's one person whom I speak with daily, and she's not technically human anymore. Lady Charlotte haunts this place, but I believe haunt is too strong of a word. She is, my dear diary, the most stubborn, delightful, precocious, and intelligent woman I have ever met. Had I been thirty years younger, I might have attempted to break her curse, if it had been as simple as loving her. But I discovered it was much more complicated than that. Alas, she has proved more of a thorn in my side than a helpmeet, so I will leave her fate to another man's courage.

Sean kept reading page after page, incredulous at his uncle's interactions with Lady Charlotte. She was quite demanding in ordering McKinley about how to care for the manor. She was very particular in how he was to care for the rose garden. She even played mean tricks on the museum visitors if she was annoyed at something McKinley had failed to do.

At one point, McKinley had described her. *So he had seen her!* Sean eagerly read on.

Her portrait at the base of the stairs does the woman no justice. Lady Charlotte is a lovely woman, if only her temper didn't get in the way of someone offering her affection. One moment, she looks like an angel; the next her blue eyes are sharp enough to pierce a man's heart straight through.

By the time Sean finished reading the pages of the diary, he was convinced that his great-uncle was not a madman. Eccentric, maybe, but not mad. At least, in his mind, he truly believed Lady Charlotte was real. There were too many things he'd written about Lady Charlotte that couldn't be easily dismissed. And Sean intended to find out the truth. McKinley had mentioned that her room was in the attic, so here Sean was.

In the attic, talking to a woman he couldn't see.

Either that, or he was certifiably schizophrenic.

Sean knew Lady Charlotte was looking at him, and she'd just demanded that he explain himself. Perhaps he shouldn't have brought up the fact that she was a bit notorious for her temper. But here he stood, talking to a ghost in the middle of the night.

"I found my uncle's diary," he said.

She didn't respond, and he had no idea if she was even still there.

At last she said, "I didn't know he kept a diary."

He was about to ask how she could miss such a thing while living in the same house as the man for years, but Sean refrained. "He wrote quite a bit about you," he said. "It seemed you had quite a close relationship, although a bit tempestuous at times."

The woman's voice scoffed.

Sean cracked a smile. She was entertaining, to say the least. "He was complimentary though, some of the time."

Another scoff.

"Would you like to read it?" Sean asked, holding out the diary that he'd carried up to the attic level with him.

It all happened so fast that Sean wasn't sure *what* exactly had happened. One minute he was holding out the diary in front of him, and the next minute, it had been swept from his hand. He'd felt a rush of air as if someone had brushed past him, but he couldn't exactly describe the sensation. He'd also smelled ... roses. She smelled like roses.

Sean closed his eyes. Was his mind playing tricks on him because of what he'd read in McKinley's diary about Lady Charlotte smelling like the roses she loved so much?

Or had Sean really smelled them? Whatever it was, the scent lingered.

He turned his attention to the small credenza below the window. The pages were slowly being flipped.

Sean's heart thumped quite hard, and he moved back toward the bed and sat down on it. He barely noticed the puff of dust that floated upward. He was mesmerized by the sight of the diary pages turning one at a time. Lady Charlotte was a fast reader, or perhaps she was skimming, looking for something specific.

He couldn't help but wonder what she looked like, sitting there, or was she standing, leaning over the credenza?

"Your uncle certainly has his own sense of humor," Lady Charlotte said in a dry tone. "It seems that his point of view was quite different than mine."

Sean nodded. "That's usually the case. Although I didn't know him that well, I do remember him being full of grandiose ideas."

The book snapped shut, and Sean flinched. Was this where he'd see her infamous temper? He was having a hard enough time digesting the fact that he was hanging out with a ghost, least of all a ghost with anger management problems. Not that he entirely blamed her—from the diary and other comments she'd made, it seemed she wasn't happy about her current residence.

"Your uncle was a difficult man," the voice said. This time it sounded closer.

Was she no longer by the credenza? The diary remained on the desk.

"But he was also a gentleman," she said, her tone softening. "And I miss his quirky ways."

Sean relaxed, but only slightly. How relaxed could he truly be in this situation? "I'm sorry about his death," Sean said. "And I'm sorry about all the changes it must mean for you as well."

"You apologize a lot, Sean McKinley."

So she knew his name. He wasn't exactly surprised. "You might call me Sean," he ventured. "May I call you . . . Charlotte?"

Something brushed the sleeve of his shirt. Not exactly a touch, more like a presence. Was she sitting by him? Every one of his senses went on alert, and he almost imagined hearing her breathing. The rose scent was stronger.

"You may not call me by only my first name," she said. "It's a familiarity that you don't have."

Sean registered the firmness in her voice, though he held back a smile. She was a ghost, but she still insisted on nineteenth-century proprieties. "You're right," Sean said. "My apologies."

A slice of air brushed against his neck, and he thought he heard a soft laugh.

"Are you laughing at me?" he asked.

"You apologize incessantly," she replied. "I'm not sure if it's amusing or annoying."

"Is that a fault?"

She seemed to hesitate. "Not exactly, I suppose. But like I said, it might grow tiresome."

A smile played at his mouth. "Will you let me know, then? When it grows tiresome?"

The rose scent grew stronger. Was she leaning closer?

When she didn't answer, he blurted out, "Do you know you smell like roses?"

"You—you can smell me?"

"I can," Sean confirmed.

"Did you know . . . ," she started to say, sounding farther away than she had previously. "Your uncle could smell roses, too, when I came into any room he occupied."

Sean nodded. He'd read as much. "I guess that makes it all very convenient. You can no longer sneak up on me."

She laughed. It was a musical laugh, one that warmed him from the inside out, one that made him laugh, too. He couldn't ever remember genuinely laughing like this with Michele. She'd never considered anything he said all that funny. It was refreshing, he thought.

He remained sitting on the bed as they talked until the night sky softened to blue, then transformed to violet.

"The sun is coming up," Lady Charlotte said. "We've talked all night."

Sean could hardly believe it. He wasn't even sure what exactly they'd talked about. Most of it had been banter. He'd told her about his family, about his younger sister Eloise who was in law school, and about how their parents had died in a car accident a couple of years ago. He'd told her about his construction company in Colorado, and about his upcoming marriage to Michele.

Charlotte had told him about previous tenants and owners and their quirky habits.

They'd laughed a lot.

43

"Sean!" Michele's voice echoed throughout the house, although it was more of a panicked screech.

"I should go," Sean said, looking to his left, seeing nothing but the window beyond and the promise of a cloudless blue day. But Lady Charlotte's voice had been coming from that direction most recently.

"She doesn't sound happy," Lady Charlotte said in a light tone.

"You would find that funny." Sean felt that he knew Lady Charlotte much better now. Yes, she was emotional, and at times temperamental. But mostly she was trapped, bored, and suffering.

"Where are you, Sean?" Michele screeched again. If Sean didn't hurry, she'd wake up the entire village.

"I'm coming down," he called back. Then he patted the bed beside him. If it was her leg, perhaps Lady Charlotte would understand the gesture.

He hurried across the room and through the doorway. Before he reached the top of the stairs that led down to the second floor, the attic bedroom shut with a soft click, followed by the sound of the lock turning.

CHAPTER 6

AFTER CHARLOTTE LOCKED the attic bedroom door, she stepped through the wall and followed Sean down the stairs. He didn't need to know how nosy she was; in fact, he didn't need to know how much their talk had meant to her. He couldn't even see her, yet he listened to every word she'd said. Teasing sometimes, yes, but mostly sharing.

Too bad Michele had to wake up and ruin everything. But Charlotte was determined to be mature about it all. Sean was engaged to be married. He'd told her that he and Michele had been a couple since high school. They'd been best friends since grade school. They'd always been together, and they always would be.

Charlotte liked the way Sean smelled, too. He wasn't wearing any of that fancy cologne some men wore, but he smelled clean, like the outdoors and fresh air. He smelled . . . alive.

By the time Sean got to the first floor of the manor, Michele was waiting for him, her arms folded, her eyes looking like she hadn't slept at all. Frankly, Charlotte felt sorry for a woman who woke up looking like a gopher stuck in a hole. Not very attractive, especially if she hadn't quite yet caught her man.

"Where have you been?" Michele said, her voice bordering on hysteria. "Why did you leave me? I couldn't find you, and you didn't answer!"

Sean hurried the last few steps to Michele and placed his hands on her shoulders. "I'm right here," he said in a soothing tone. "Where would I go? I was just checking some things out."

Michele pulled away from him, her eyes darting toward the painting hanging on the wall at the bottom of the stairs. "We can't stay here. That painting blinked at me!"

Sean seemed to hesitate. "You're really tired, Michele. It's been a long trip. Let's get some coffee going."

But Michele was one stubborn woman. In fact, she reminded Charlotte of her own mother. When she got an idea in her head, there was no dissuading her.

"I don't want coffee *here*," Michele complained. She sounded less hysterical now. "I want to get out of here, and I don't care where we go. We can stay with that Farland man."

Charlotte stiffened. This manor was perfectly capable of hosting guests. They didn't need to resort to Farland's run-down farmhouse. Besides, there was a bed-and-breakfast by the pub. Perhaps Michele could leave and Sean could stay . . .

"Michele," Sean said in a sterner voice than Charlotte had heard him use before. She was quite proud to hear it now. "We're not going anywhere. We're going to make coffee and finish what we came here to do."

Charlotte was glad Sean was sticking up for himself, but she felt deflated all the same. He was still planning to leave, and he wasn't throwing Michele out.

Michele bit her lip and turned. She practically stomped into the kitchen, then she banged things around, apparently making that coffee. *Americans.*

Sean was in less of a hurry to get to the kitchen. In fact, he turned around and looked at the stairs where Charlotte was standing. She knew he couldn't see her. But . . . her heart seemed to expand when he winked.

He knew she was there.

"Roses," he whispered, then turned and walked into the kitchen.

Charlotte couldn't move. She literally felt as if her eyes might fill with happy tears. It was quite foolish and sentimental, really. But she was starting to like Sean. A lot. He was sweet, patient, intelligent, amusing, handsome, charming, and . . . engaged.

Blast.

She waited, and almost flinched when the voice came: *Charlotte!*

She grinned. "Yes, Mother?" she whispered. Nothing else was spoken, of course. Somewhere, through the sphere that separated the living from the dead, her mother was paying attention. For some reason, this gave Charlotte the courage that she might not have otherwise had—the courage to go into Michele and Sean's room and take all the pillows off the bed. She shoved them under the bed, sure that they would encounter plenty of dust balls.

Let the games begin, Charlotte decided.

Sean could keep Michele here all he wanted, but ultimately it would be up to Michele whether she stayed or not. Charlotte just hoped that when all was said and done, Sean would realize that Michele wasn't the woman for him.

Not that Charlotte thought Sean could be the one for *her*—the one to break the curse. She couldn't even speculate on that because then she'd get her hopes up as she had in the past. But Sean deserved someone better than a weak, demanding, spoiled woman.

So, as Charlotte glided from the bedroom, she couldn't quite feel guilty about hiding all the pillows. Then she hesitated in the foyer. Sean and Michele were in the kitchen, and apparently she'd calmed down, because they were talking in low tones. Sean would know she'd hidden the pillows. She'd told him about her tricks. Would he be upset? Would he think less of her?

She was about to return to the bedroom and pull the pillows back out, dust and all, when she heard a car coming up the long driveway.

It was faint, but distinct. Charlotte forgot about the pillow dilemma and hurried to the front door and stepped through it. She didn't recognize the dark green car approaching. But she did know she didn't like all of these changes.

A lone man was inside the car, and he pulled up to the base of the broad steps and climbed out. He looked down at a piece of paper in his hand, then back up at the manor.

"Someone's here," Sean said from inside the house.

Moments later, he opened the door and stepped past Charlotte.

"You've brought my suitcase?" Sean bounded down the steps.

"Good day," the driver said, flashing a smile.

Sean hurried toward him, stopped and shook his hand, then reached into the trunk that the driver had opened.

"Thanks so much," Sean said. "Would you like to come in? We just made coffee."

Charlotte turned to see the other half of the "we" that Sean was referring to. Michele had come to stand in the doorway. She looked much calmer and actually quite pretty in a disheveled sort of way.

"Yes, come on in," Michele said in a perfectly friendly voice. No one would have guessed that she'd been a raving maniac moments ago.

Interestingly enough, the driver looked up again at the manor, as if he were counting the number of stories. Or perhaps he was checking out the state of the roof like Sean had the day before. What was up with these men? The roof was fine.

"This is Breken Manor, right?" the driver said.

"Yes, and he's the new owner," Michele pointed out, quite unnecessarily in Charlotte's opinion. "We're going to sell it, though." She shuddered—actually shuddered.

"Uh," the driver said. "Yes, I think I'm good. I'm not too keen on haunted places."

Charlotte stared at the driver, boring holes into him that he wasn't even aware of. Unfortunately. Get him inside, and she could show him a thing or two. But out here, there wasn't much she could do but blow a scoop of dirt into his face.

"See!" Michele said, pointing a finger at Sean. "The old man, and now *this* guy. Both of them said it's haunted!" She turned her now wide eyes upon the driver. "This house gives me the creeps. Do you know a good place to stay around here?"

"Uh," the driver said. The expression was apparently a habit for him, Charlotte decided. This time he raised his hands as if he were devoid of having any advice or opinion at all. "I'm not from around here. I heard about this place from a friend of mine who used to go to school in the village. He said that the ghost is one angry wo—"

Charlotte was upon the man so fast that he didn't have a chance to finish his sentence. She passed right through him, which she knew would chill him to the bone. It wasn't her favorite activity, and she only did it when desperate. She was desperately furious right now.

The driver stumbled back, and then he started to hyperventilate.

Charlotte stepped away and placed her hands on her hips. She watched as he gasped for air and reached for the door handle to the car as if he were a drowning victim.

"What's wrong?" Michele called out.

Sean moved forward and grabbed the guy's arm. "Are you all right?"

The driver pulled away from Sean's grasp. "Leave me alone," he practically yelled before sliding into the driver's seat and slamming the door shut.

"Wait!" Sean yelled as the tires spun, spewing dirt

and gravel against the lower steps. "I've got a tip to give you."

But the driver hadn't heard him, or didn't care. He slammed down on the gas pedal and peeled out, tires squealing.

Sean and Michele stared after the car. Michele's mouth was hanging open. Sean's face was flushed. As the car turned onto the main road, still sounding like it was in the race of its life, Sean spun around.

Uh oh.

Although there was a good three meters between them, Charlotte stepped back.

Sean's eyes were searching for her. She knew it.

"What did you do?" he shouted. "What did you do to that guy?"

"Who are you talking to?" Michele asked from the top of the stairs. Her voice was back to rising panic mode.

Sean ignored her. "Charlotte! What did you do?"

"*Lady* Charlotte," she corrected. It perhaps wasn't the best timing, but it was habit.

Sean turned, facing her as if he could see her.

Charlotte actually felt his gaze. It was uncanny.

"Dammit, Charlotte," Sean said. "You've got to stop this. First Michele, now that man. What do you think he'll tell everyone he knows? I'm trying to *sell* this place. He wouldn't even *come inside for coffee!*"

Sean was yelling at her. He was livid. And Charlotte felt about as small as an ant.

Michele had started crying, covering her mouth as if she'd just witnessed a cruel beheading. What was wrong with these people? The driver had been rude. Charlotte had only played a very small prank. And now Sean was acting like it was the *Titanic* all over again.

Well, if he wanted to be angry, it should be at her *mother* for casting the curse. Yet Charlotte didn't want anyone else to be angry with her mother. She reserved that for herself.

Charlotte wouldn't cry. She wouldn't give that power to Sean, or his obnoxious fiancée. Charlotte strode right past him, her head held high. She didn't care that she brushed against his arm, and that he flinched at the sensation. And then, to spite them all, she floated straight up, toward the roof. She entered the window of the attic room, grateful to be alone at last.

And only then did she let herself cry.

CHAPTER 7

SEAN STARED AT the ground where the airline employee's car had spun out before he practically had a heart attack and almost dropped dead right in front of the manor. Michele was crying again and speaking rapidly about something. He couldn't even understand her if he tried. When she cried, her words were incoherent.

But he'd understood Lady Charlotte's words perfectly. She'd done something to spook the man. Sean had then lost his temper and started yelling at an invisible woman, and now Michele was freaking out. Not that he could blame her.

"Oh my gosh, oh my gosh, you've lost your mind!" Michele cried.

Sean snapped out of whatever weird existence he'd been focused on and hurried up the stairs. "Michele, I'm sorry," he started. "Listen to me, babe. I need to show you a diary that my uncle wrote. Everything will make sense then."

He reached for her, wanting to offer her some comfort.

"Don't touch me," Michele said, backing up through the doorway. She held her hands in front of her as if to ward off an evil spirit.

Again, Sean didn't blame her.

She turned and ran through the house. Before he could get over the threshold, she'd slammed, and most likely locked, the door of the bedroom they'd stayed in the night before.

"Michele!" Sean hurried to the bedroom and tried the doorknob. Yep, it was locked. "Michele, listen to me. I can explain everything." He couldn't exactly explain it, but he could at least tell her what he read in the diary and about the conversation with Charlotte. Yes, that was right. He was dropping the "Lady." They were in the twenty-first century, and she'd just have to accept it.

Sean leaned his head against the door. He could hear Michele muttering something and a lot of movement going on. Was she packing?

"Please open the door," Sean said. "Give me two minutes to explain. What you saw, or *heard*, isn't what you think it was." Sort of. "Please."

Michele didn't answer. He heard the occasional hiccupping sob, and he hoped she was calming down.

"Michele?" he asked in a perfectly calm tone. The adrenaline that had been pulsing madly through him was now draining away.

"Ahhh!" she screeched.

Sean flinched. "Michele!" He banged on the door. "What's wrong now?"

"The pillows!" she yelled. "Where are the pillows?"

He heard something crash to the floor, and then the door flew open. Michele stood there, her face blotched with tears, her chest heaving. "Did you move the pillows?"

Sean stared at her, feeling the color drain from his face. He looked past Michele to see the bed stripped of all pillows. His gaze involuntarily went to the base of the bed, where he knew, *knew*, that Charlotte had hidden them. Uncle McKinley had said it was one of her pranks in his diary, and Charlotte herself had told him about it with a laugh. Sean had laughed with her.

He wasn't laughing now.

Michele clamped a hand over her mouth. "Oh my gosh, oh my gosh." She lunged for her suitcase and zipped it shut, catching an article of clothing in the zipper in the process. She didn't seem to notice. Pushing past Sean, she dragged the suitcase through the hallway, across the foyer, and out the front door.

Sean followed. "Wait, what are you doing?"

Michele looked back at him. "I'm leaving," she said, her voice trembling. She wiped at the tears on her face. "Bring me the car keys. I'll never step foot in that . . . place, again." She spat the last few words. She hefted the suitcase over to the car, which was locked, of course.

Sean exhaled. He could get in the car with her. They could drive around, and she'd calm down, and then he could explain everything. He hurried into the house, then into the kitchen, looking for the keys. Not seeing them, he went into the foyer again, scanning the empty hall table. Maybe the bedroom? He strode into the bedroom. Nothing.

Kneeling down, he peeked under the bed. Sure enough, there were all the pillows. What was Charlotte thinking? After their long night together, talking and what he thought was enjoying each other's company, she did this.

Sean stood up and took a final glance about the room. There was only one more place to check; well, two, but he didn't want to think about the second place. He left the bedroom and made his way to the library where he'd found the journal. No keys on the desk, and no keys in the drawers that he'd opened.

So, it seemed he was going up to the attic.

He didn't dare tell Michele that he'd be any longer. She wouldn't come back inside the house, and hopefully she wasn't currently dragging her suitcase down the driveway to the main road.

Sean took the stairs two at a time, and when he reached the attic door at the top of the stairs, he was sure that Charlotte had heard him coming.

And of course the door was locked.

"Charlotte," he said through the door. "I need the car keys, and I know you have them."

No sound.

He knocked. This was complete déjà vu. Knocking on the door and trying to get the woman on the other side to open it.

"Charlotte, we need to talk about some things," he said. "But first, I need to find a place for Michele to stay. She's completely hysterical, thanks to you."

"Just Michele?" a voice said right next to his ear. "Not you? You're coming back?"

Sean turned, seeing nothing, but he knew she was close.

"I'm coming back," he said in a measured tone. He had to hurry all of this up. Get the keys. Find a place to set up Michele. Then he could sort all of this out with Charlotte later. "Please, *Lady* Charlotte."

He waited. Finally the door opened and there, on the desk, was the closed diary and his car keys sitting on top of the book. He grabbed the keys, then hesitated in the doorway. Turning back, he grabbed the diary. Charlotte didn't say anything. "Thank you," he said to the empty attic room. He hurried down the stairs and outside where, thankfully, Michele was still waiting.

"Found them," he said, avoiding looking at her directly in the eyes. There would be plenty of time for that later. He unlocked the car and lifted her suitcase inside. Then he climbed in. By the time he sat down, Michele was already in the passenger seat, staring straight ahead, her arms folded.

Sean didn't say anything until they reached the main road. "Here, read this," he said, handing her the diary. "Just a couple of pages. My uncle wrote it, and I believe him . . . obviously."

Michele took the book and sniffled, but at least she opened it. As he drove, she turned pages. By the time they reached the village center, she'd read through several pages already. Sean parked in front of a pub.

"So?" he said.

Michele looked over at him. Her eyes were dry, her face less blotchy now.

"You told me your uncle had some sort of mental

illness," Michele said. "He covered it up with his eccentricity, and people in your family just went along with it, basically by staying out of his way, since he had his own money to spend."

Sean nodded, although he didn't quite know where she was going with this.

"Something's wrong with that house, and I don't know what it is." She blinked rapidly. "At first I thought it was haunted, and this . . . this Charlotte person is really a ghost. But when you were inside the house taking fifteen minutes to get the keys that were right in plain sight, I remembered the things you'd said about your great-uncle." She looked away from him and went silent.

"And?" Sean prompted. Might as well get this all out.

She shook her head, then handed over the diary. "This diary confirms it. Sean, your great-uncle was *insane*. The painting, the driver . . . those were weird, but the painting was a trick of the light. The driver was already spooked by stories he'd heard. I just can't explain how you think it's normal to talk to someone who's not real, who's not even there."

"I didn't say it was normal," Sean said. "Did you read what McKinley said?" He tapped the diary. "I read it last night, and I went up to the attic. That's where the ghost lady hangs out. She talked to me, and I could hear her." He threw up his hands. "I'm kind of freaking out here, too—I mean a few hours ago, I would have agreed with you one hundred percent. But, now . . . I can't deny what I've seen and heard."

Michele's gaze was full of pity. "That's just the thing, Sean. I think you need help. A psychiatrist or something.

Medication maybe. You don't need to be ashamed. You know I love you, and it's hard to hear this, but someone needs to tell you."

"Michele—"

"I need to say this," she cut in. "It's for your own good. The last few months—ever since we've been engaged, actually—you haven't been yourself. You've been forgetting things. You've been too caught up in learning about your crazy uncle. It's like you're channeling him in some way. You're . . ." Her voice broke. "You're no longer the man I want to marry."

Sean felt as if he'd been kicked in the stomach. He stared at Michele. "What the hell? You're breaking up with me because Breken Manor is haunted? Ask anyone in this village about it, and see what they say! Is everyone else crazy, too?"

Michele merely pursed her lips and waited for him to stop ranting. He said a few more choice things, then she popped open her door. "Like I said, I'm sorry to have to tell you the truth." Her voice trembled. "This all didn't start with Breken Manor, although I'm not surprised it's been a huge trigger. Just know that I only want to help you, to support you. When you get back to the States, I'll be there with my family ready to help you get the right treatment." She twisted her engagement ring off her finger and handed it over.

Sean could only stare at the diamond ring in disbelief. Michele was breaking up with him. She dropped the ring into the cup holder, then she opened her door all the way. She sniffled, then shut the door. Sean couldn't move, feeling completely numb while she tugged her suitcase out of the back seat, then wheeled it toward the pub.

Sean was still in the car, staring at nothing, when she came out of the pub and wheeled the suitcase along the sidewalk. He looked at her then, walking away. He watched her walk into what looked like a bed-and-breakfast. One part of him wanted to go after her.

The other part of him wanted to let her go. She'd come to her senses; she had to. He couldn't believe that she was really going to head back to the States without him. In an hour or two, she'd be calling him to apologize.

So, Sean backed out of the parking place and drove back to Breken Manor to meet whatever fate awaited him.

CHAPTER 8

CHARLOTTE HEARD THE car before she saw it. Sean was back, and he was alone. She was at first supremely happy about that. He must have gotten Michele a room at the bed-and-breakfast, and now . . .

Sean climbed out of the car and looked straight up at her attic window as if he knew she was spying on him. He didn't look happy.

Uh oh.

Charlotte had been yelled at enough for today. Enough to last her for quite a while, in fact. She hurried down the stairs and went out into the gardens behind the house. Let Sean go to the attic; she wouldn't be there.

Although she was wondering what was happening with Michele, Charlotte didn't think she could bear watching Sean pack up his things and lock the manor back up.

Perhaps Sean would decide to sell the place as is, and she'd never see him again. Charlotte immersed herself in the rose garden, checking the new buds and tearing off wilting petals and letting them flutter away in the light breeze.

She could hear Sean trying to get her attention. First his voice sounded from the attic, and then he diligently searched each room, calling for her. She hadn't realized she'd been hoping he'd come outside.

"Charlotte!" he said from the back patio. "Are you in the garden?"

Despite herself, her heart soared.

Yet, she said nothing. Sean trudged into the garden, walking right past her. He slowed when he reached the end of the first row of rose bushes.

"I don't know why you're not answering me," he said. He bent over a group of particularly full blooms and breathed in. "I know you're close by. I can smell you."

"You're *in* a rose garden!" Charlotte said, then clamped her mouth shut.

"Aha!" Sean said, lifting his head. He didn't look angry anymore. In fact, he looked like a cross between amused and . . . sad. "You *are* here."

Charlotte didn't move. Sean was perhaps two meters away from her. Any closer, and she would have wanted to step back. This new expression on his face did something new to her heart—it felt like compassion.

"I'm sorry about Michele," she blurted out. She hadn't meant to apologize. That was so unlike her, more like something Sean would do—when he wasn't yelling at her in anger.

Sean rubbed the side of his face. "You have no idea what you set into motion."

Again, his words weren't angry, or bitter—only sad.

It made Charlotte feel horribly guilty, and that was quite another new sensation for her.

Sean reached into his pocket and fished something out. When he opened his hand, a diamond ring sparkled in the sun against his palm.

Charlotte stared.

"She gave it back," Sean said. "Told me I was insane like my uncle. She doesn't want to be married to a man who talks to ghosts, I guess."

Charlotte's eyes burned, and her throat tightened. She didn't know whether to rage against Michele, or cry over Sean, or both.

"I'm not certain that I'd believe in ghosts, either," she started.

"If you weren't one?" Sean asked, one side of his mouth lifting into a sad half smile.

"Exactly," she said. *Goodness.* She was feeling horrible, so horrible. Had Sean been very much in love with Michele? Of course he had! Why would she think of such a thing except to ease her own conscience? But the fact of the matter was, she'd caused their breakup.

"Perhaps you'd better go back to your country," she said. "You should repair your relationship with your fiancée and return to your job, your sister, and all that you know." She waved a hand about the rose garden, even though Sean couldn't see. "This place will sell to some treasure hunting enthusiast. Who knows, maybe the ghostly legend of Lady Charlotte will attract thrill seekers."

Sean didn't say anything. He just fingered the petals on one of the pink roses. Charlotte liked that he was standing in her garden, appreciating her roses. But she still didn't like the sadness on his face. It was like he was giving up on something he'd wanted very much.

"Michele will come to her senses," Charlotte tried again. "She won't be able to stay away from you very long. I mean, look at you, Sean McKinley. You're a catch if I've ever seen one. During my lifetime, we would have called you a *very eligible bachelor.* And perhaps a bit of a rake."

"A *rake?*" Sean looked up from the flower. "You would have called me a garden tool?"

Charlotte laughed. "Not exactly. A rake is a man, who . . . well, who is fond of the women. He's charming, devastatingly handsome, and doesn't settle down until he marries. And even then, he might have a wandering eye. For what woman, married or otherwise, can resist him?"

Sean lifted a single brow. A gesture that Charlotte had not seen until now. Her ghostly heart fluttered, and she might have swooned back in the day of tight corsets and near-starvation diets.

"You think I'm 'charming and devastatingly handsome'?" he asked.

Well. Charlotte felt hot. Extremely hot. Which was saying a great deal. Ghosts did not overheat; or apparently they did in rose gardens standing just a short distance from charming and devastatingly handsome men. "You are nice-looking."

Sean's other eyebrow went up. "That's not what you said before."

64

"I might be dead," she said. "But I'm not blind."

Sean laughed, and Charlotte smiled. A sort of embarrassed smile.

When he stopped laughing, he took several steps forward. "Where are you, Charlotte?"

"*Lady* Charlotte," she automatically corrected.

Another step. He was actually only an arm's distance away now. "Here's the thing, *dear lady*," he said in a quiet voice. "I've had to make quite a few concessions in regards to you. I've traveled all this way only to find that the house I inherited is occupied by *a ghost*. I've had to explain to my ex-fiancée why I'm not crazy, which she actually doesn't believe, so she dumped me. And now I'm back here again, trying to figure out what my next step should be. So, I've decided that I will call you Charlotte. *I* own this house now, and therefore, I'm the master of it. So, whether or not you like it, dear ghost, it's the twenty-first century, and you're living in *my* house. That means that I get to decide what to call the woman who completely upended my life."

Charlotte was a bit breathless, as far as ghost breathing went. And she was hot again. Those deep green eyes of his were staring right into hers—as if he knew exactly how tall she was. It was quite disconcerting.

The only thing she could say after that speech was: "All right."

"All right?" he asked.

"Yes," she whispered.

He lifted a hand, reaching toward her. "You're right in front of me, aren't you?"

She nodded, then said, "I am."

Sean continued to lift his hand. He was touching her, or would have been if she'd been flesh and blood. His hand trailed along her invisible arm, and she reached for his fingers, to link them together. But he didn't seem to feel her touch, and his hand slid away from hers.

"I could smell you in a garden full of roses," he said. "So why can't I see you?"

He was so close.

She leaned toward him until she could hear his heart beating. It was so strong and alive. It was also beating fast. She closed her eyes, just listening to his breathing and his heartbeat. She missed being alive. She missed feeling human touch. She missed someone actually looking at her.

He wasn't moving. It was as if he knew she was listening to him.

What if . . . what if she showed herself to him? *No.* She'd known Old McKinley for years before she allowed him to see her. Sean could be gone next week, or even tomorrow. It was too personal of a thing to share with a man she'd never see again. And she knew it would make her feel connected to him, and then she would grieve over him when he left.

"What are you going to do, Sean?" she asked.

"Hmm?" he said, in sort of a daze. He blinked a couple of times and shoved his hands in his pockets. "I'm going to get some repairs done while I wait to see what happens with the listing. If it sells quickly enough, I can sign all the paperwork before heading back to the States."

Charlotte listened to every word, but all she comprehended was that she still had more time with Sean. That was a good thing, right? She knew he'd be leaving soon. And as long as she remembered that, her heart was in no danger.

And who knew? Michele seemed like a temperamental person, and she could come sweeping back in and scoop Sean up again.

"So," Sean said. "I'm going to rummage up something to eat from one of those tin cans I saw and get to work."

"I'll be out here until dark," she told him. She didn't know why she was telling him.

He nodded and started back toward the house. She didn't move as she watched him cross the patio and disappear inside. She liked him in her house. She liked that he'd come to the rose garden to find her. And she liked that he could still smell her when he was standing in the middle of it.

Sean McKinley was a man she'd regret saying goodbye to.

CHAPTER 9

SEAN STOOD AT the base of the stairs, looking at the portrait of Charlotte. Perhaps it was because he'd seen this painting before he heard her voice that he pictured her exactly as she sat in the portrait. Her blue eyes seemed filled with knowledge, even amusement, as if she were teasing him. *Or torturing him.*

He didn't understand Charlotte. She'd been haunting this place for decades, yet no man had fallen in love with her to break the curse. And how would it all work exactly? Would the man declare his eternal love, and Charlotte would float on up to heaven? Or dissipate forever?

His gaze trailed along the red tones of her hair mixed with honey blonde. Even in today's world, with no makeup, she'd be a beauty. A tragedy, really, that she'd died so young. Never mind the curse.

He'd never asked her how she'd died. Was it poor manners to ask a ghost about her means of death? Sean

69

shook his head to dispel his thoughts. Here he was, debating with himself about what to ask a ghost ... A ghost!

It was impossible, unbelievable, to even consider that a ghost was real. Yet, she was real.

He wondered what she'd be wearing if he could see her. The white dress with the blue trim in the painting was what he imagined. His uncle hadn't described her clothing. And her eyes—Sean stared into her eyes as if he could force her to look back at him. They were anything but serene; more like she was testing, or challenging, the painter to do a decent job at his craft. Sean had the feeling that Charlotte's personality hadn't changed much over the centuries.

This made him smile, despite himself, and despite how angry he'd been with the situation with Michele. He closed his eyes and blew out a breath. Maybe Michele was right. Maybe he had changed.

If Sean was completely honest with himself, he was more intrigued with a woman who had been dead over 150 years than his own fiancée. Opening his eyes, he once again gazed into the blue eyes of Charlotte. Perhaps Michele was right. He was going crazy.

He left the foyer and walked into the kitchen. His notebook was on the table, untouched by Charlotte. Picking it up, he thumbed through his notes. First things first, he needed to make a few calls. About an hour later, he had a roofer lined up. He told the roofer he'd pay him extra if he could start the next day and do a rush job.

Sean headed out to the old barn that he hadn't taken the time to check out yet. He hoped to find some tools and supplies. He supposed it had at one time housed horses belonging to the owners of the manor. But when he stepped inside what looked to be a completely run-down barn, he was surprised to see that it was quite clean inside. And orderly. The scent of hay lingered, although the floor had been cleared of any hay.

Three horse stalls lined one wall. They'd been cleaned out, too, and although the wood was old, it was still in good shape, as if the barn walls had preserved it against rain and sun. A long table ran against the other side of the barn, and upon it Sean found a couple of boxes of nails and screws, a few tools, and some cans of paint. He collected a hammer, a screwdriver, and the box of screws, intent on fixing the loose cupboards in the kitchen.

When he returned to the kitchen, there was no evidence, or scent, of Charlotte's presence, so Sean got to work. Every so often he'd pause and check his phone log.

Michele still hadn't called or texted. He was still in a bit of a fog about all that had happened. It was almost like she had just been waiting for an excuse to break things off, which was strange because she'd been the one to pressure *him* into marriage. And the times in the past when he'd suggested they take a break, she'd become so hysterical that he hadn't the heart to go through with it.

Now, here he was, starting repairs on a house he'd never live in, with the companionship of a ghost. Well, Michele knew how to reach him if she wanted to have an honest conversation. Although the longer she waited to contact him, the more he thought the breakup might be best for both of them.

As he worked, his mind kept returning to Charlotte. He wondered about her life, and her cause of death, and what exactly the curse was all about. He found himself more focused on Charlotte and her problems than the fact that his own relationship had fallen apart that morning.

When he'd finished securing and repairing the kitchen cupboards, he walked into the library where he'd found his uncle's diary. The place smelled musty, like old books, not like roses. Charlotte wasn't here, either. It seemed she'd made good on her promise to stay outside in the gardens.

Sean spent the next hour or so looking through the books on the shelves. Behind a row of books, he found one volume wedged in the corner, as if it had been long forgotten. It appeared to be a history of the village. Sitting down, he browsed through it, not finding anything that related specifically to Charlotte until the very end. There was an entire chapter on the "Ghost of Breken Manor."

Born in 1840, Lady Charlotte Breken was said to be the illegitimate daughter of Ernest II, a German king who also happened to be the brother of Prince Albert. With Ernest II betrothed to Princess Alexandrine of Baden, Ernest made it a point to secure away his mistress, Lady Constance Breken, and her unborn child. The illegitimate child, Charlotte, was born in hiding, and although Constance made repeated attempts to establish her daughter into English Society, Ernest II refused to acknowledge her or make her legal.

When Lady Breken and her daughter were in a

serious carriage accident together, Lady Breken knew she was not long for the world. Upon her deathbed, Lady Breken swore that if her daughter died due to this tragic accident and was deprived of finding the love of her life like Lady Breken had been, Charlotte would forever haunt the Breken Manor and all those who dwelled therein. Her curse could only be broken with the full repentance and apology of Ernest II, and when the owner of the manor declared his true and sincere love for her.

These two actions would make all that had gone wrong, right, in the mind of Lady Breken. Only then would Lady Charlotte be freed.

Sean couldn't read any more for a moment. He now knew how Charlotte had died. And he knew that Charlotte was technically royalty, although an illegitimate daughter. Now he could understand Lady Breken's anger more easily. This manor house was a far cry from any royal palace. Still, Lady Breken seemed to be a selfish woman, and she had only added more of a burden upon her daughter. It was hardly fair to Charlotte. Her parents' deceptions had not been her fault, yet she'd been made to pay for them in the most convoluted way.

He continued to read, learning that Charlotte had died hours after her own mother. It wasn't but a week later that the first report of a ghost at Breken Manor emerged when a relative of Ernest II came to look over the house and offer it to a buyer.

The rest of the article went through the names of the various owners and the dates of acquisitions. It was an interesting list but held no meaning for Sean. Although Charlotte would likely know every name.

He leaned back in his chair, thinking of how a "curse" could truly have power. Apparently it had worked, because Sean was a witness to Charlotte's continued existence. Looking through more books in the library, he didn't find anything else that related directly to Charlotte or her mother.

Sean set the history book on the desk, then went into the bedroom, where he lay down on the bed just as the sun was setting. He didn't even bother with getting the pillows from under the bed. They'd probably be dusty anyway. He closed his eyes, expecting sleep to come quickly, but instead, he mulled over the life, and death, and curse of Charlotte Breken.

CHAPTER 10

CHARLOTTE WATCHED SEAN sleep. She knew she shouldn't, but she couldn't help it. She'd stayed outside in the garden until the sun set. Then, expecting him to be in the kitchen, perhaps eating something out of another tin, she entered the house quietly. Not that she wasn't normally quiet, but she didn't want to get close enough to him that he might smell her.

Sean wasn't in the kitchen, so Charlotte paused outside the bedroom. He'd left the door open, and she could hear his even breathing. It wasn't even quite dark, but he'd been awake for a long time.

Charlotte's phantom heart seemed to swell as she thought about him. She really shouldn't stand here while he was sleeping, but she didn't listen to her own reason. Moving into the bedroom, she stopped close to the bed.

Even if he opened his eyes, he wouldn't be able to see her. And if he stirred, well, she could hurry out of the room so that he couldn't smell her, either. He looked so relaxed in the soft twilight of the room. She'd heard him working on the kitchen cupboards. She'd heard him talking to himself a few times. And the curse words! Yes, she'd heard those, too.

But now all that had faded away, and he was sleeping.

His eyes opened. Charlotte froze.

He blinked and rolled over onto his back, staring up at the darkening ceiling.

"Charlotte?" he said.

She didn't answer. Maybe he was talking to himself.

"Charlotte, I know you're in here," he said, sounding exasperated. "Why are you watching me sleep?"

She'd been caught. He had a better sense of smell than a dog.

"I—I was just checking up on you," she said. "I didn't think you'd go to sleep so early."

"I live a dozen time zones away," he said. "Your day is my night." He turned his head in her direction.

"I'm sorry," she said. *Apologizing!* "I didn't mean to wake you."

He sat up and swung his legs over the edge of the bed.

She took a step back, not that he could see her action. She really wanted to step forward and smooth the muss of his hair.

"I found a book in the library that contains a history of the village," he said.

Charlotte stared at him. She hadn't expected him to talk about a book. What was he getting at? And then she knew. "It talks about *me,* doesn't it?"

"Yes," he said, not sounding entirely pleased about it.

76

When he didn't elaborate, she folded her arms, and said, "What did it say?"

He rubbed the side of his face, a gesture that she was becoming familiar with.

"It's quite revealing," he said, his voice lower now, as if he were the bearer of bad news.

Charlotte didn't like it. She was already dead, already cursed, so how bad could the news be?

"It talks about how you died," he continued. "And it lists the requirements for breaking the curse."

"Oh, that's all?" she asked, although her voice sounded a bit shaky.

Sean stood from the bed and took a couple of steps forward. "I'm really sorry, Charlotte." His voice was just above a whisper.

"You look like someone has died," she said. A bad joke. "And you really don't need to apologize. I've known about the curse my entire death, you know. There's nothing new about it."

Sean took another step closer. "I wondered how you died," he said. "But it seemed wrong to bring it up."

"It wasn't a horrible death, nor was it pleasant," Charlotte said, with an invisible shrug. "I remember the carriage veering to the side, then tipping. I hit my head and never woke up."

Sean nodded, looking at her. Or through her. "Then your mother cursed you. What a strange thing."

She said nothing. She could only nod. He'd wondered about her, and that was enough.

"Uncle McKinley said in his diary that the curse

could be broken by the owner of the house falling in love with you."

"Yes," she whispered. Her hopes were rising, and she hated herself for it.

"But, he mentioned there was something else to the curse he couldn't fulfill," Sean said in a slow voice. "And I didn't realize how significant that statement was until I read the history book."

"Something *else*?" Charlotte didn't like where this was going. She, of course hadn't heard the curse word for word. She was too busy dying in the next room. But she'd heard it repeated plenty of times by manor owners and servants throughout the generations. "What are you talking about?" The panic spreading felt real and not ghostly at all.

"In the book it says there are two things that have to be done to break it," Sean said with hesitation. "I think you should read it."

Charlotte turned away. She couldn't look into those steady green eyes of his for a moment. Had she been thinking the curse was simple all along, only to learn now that it wasn't? Perhaps she'd believed in the wrong solution all of these years. And that's why she was still here.

"Charlotte?" Sean said. "What's wrong?"

Could he guess that she was upset? "I—I'm all right," she said at last. "I suppose that I'm just nervous."

"Come on," Sean said, walking past her. "We'll read it together. I think there's more power in knowledge, don't you?"

"Yes," she said, although she could feel her nerves getting the best of her.

Sean led the way, and she followed him into the library. He turned on a single lamp. There, on the desk was a book she'd never seen before.

"Where did you find this?" she asked.

"It was wedged behind another group of books," Sean said. "Almost like someone hid it. Someone who didn't want it to be found."

Charlotte reached toward the book, and with her ghostly force, caused the cover to flip open. She didn't know if she wanted to read the words, especially if Sean was in the room. He seemed to be becoming more and more in tune with her emotions.

Sean now noticed her hesitation. "Here, I'll show you the chapter."

He nearly walked right through her, so she hurried to move over. She didn't want him to feel the deep chill that happened when she passed through someone.

Sean leaned over the desk and flipped to the end of book, then he stopped on a chapter titled "Ghost of Breken Manor."

"That's me," Charlotte said.

Sean lifted his head briefly and said, "Yes."

Charlotte started to read and then stopped. Everything inside her ghostly body felt tight and agitated, like she was being squeezed by a giant press.

"Charlotte?" Sean sounded far away, although he hadn't moved. "Do you want me to read it?"

She didn't answer for a moment. Finally, she said, "Is it so awful?"

"I'm not sure," he said. "You would know more than me."

"All right," Charlotte said. "Read it to me."

And so he did. His voice was calm, but she sensed his agitation as well. When he got to the part about the curse, Charlotte realized she was clenching her hands together, and if she'd had blood in her body, it would have drained from her face.

"Upon her deathbed, Lady Breken swore that if her daughter died due to this tragic accident and was deprived of finding the love of her life like Lady Breken had been, Charlotte would forever haunt the Breken Manor and all those who dwelled therein," Sean read. *"Her curse could only be broken with the full repentance and apology of Ernest II, and when the owner of the manor declared his true and sincere love for her.*

"These two actions would make all that had gone wrong, right in the mind of Lady Breken. Only then would Lady Charlotte be freed."

He stopped reading, and Charlotte felt as if she'd stopped feeling anything.

"Is it true?" she whispered.

"I don't know," Sean said. "I'm new to all of this."

Charlotte released a sad laugh. "I don't know, either. I thought . . . I thought the curse was . . ." She turned away from Sean as her eyes filled with invisible tears. Her body had started to shake. If the curse couldn't be broken without the "full repentance and apology of Ernest II," then Charlotte was doomed forever. Ernest II had died in

1893. And Charlotte had never heard of any sort of repentance or apology on behalf of her or her mother.

She collapsed onto the settee at one end of the library, as far as she could get from the history book. It was hopeless, completely hopeless. She'd been damned to this manor for the rest of forever. Another wave of sadness and grief rose in her, and she closed her eyes. Perhaps she'd never open them again. She'd let the living come and go, and she'd stay right here, sitting on the library settee as the world moved on without her. Maybe next time she opened her eyes, robots or aliens would have taken over the human race. But she'd still be here, on the settee, filled with misery. She hugged her arms about her and released a silent sob.

"Charlotte," Sean said. His voice sounded right in front of her.

She opened her eyes to find Sean crouching before her, his hand hovering over her knee, as if he knew exactly how she was sitting. His eyes were wide and staring, and his face had lost color.

"I can see you," Sean said in a voice filled with wonder. "You're sitting down, aren't you? And . . ." His hand lifted from her knee and hovered over her folded arms. "You're—you're wearing a purple dress."

"Lavender," she corrected.

Sean smiled. "Lavender, then." His hand moved up her arm, and although she couldn't feel a thing, she wished she could. He stopped at her shoulder. "But your eyes are definitely blue."

Her sorrow faded as she stared back at Sean. He could see her? She must have let down her defenses in her emotional state. But now she found she didn't want to put those defenses back up. She quite liked the awe-filled way Sean was looking at her.

Charlotte lifted a hand to wipe at the tears on her cheeks, and Sean lifted his hand at the same time.

"May I?" he asked.

She lowered her hand and nodded. Sean ran his finger across her cheek to wipe away the tears that had fallen. Of course, nothing happened because his human hand couldn't touch her ghostly skin. But Charlotte thought it was the most romantic experience she'd ever had. Not that Sean was in love with her or anything. And even if he was, he couldn't break the curse. No one could. Her father was dead. There was no way to get an apology from him now.

CHAPTER 11

THE WOMAN IN front of him was perhaps the most beautiful person Sean had ever seen. She was more beautiful than the painting he'd stared at aplenty. Her blue eyes did glimmer, Sean decided, and right now they were glimmering with tears. Had he done the right thing by telling her about the chapter in the history book and dashing all of her hopes?

Charlotte's honey-red hair fell around her shoulders in waves. She wore a dress that was slim fitting and floor length, with a low neckline that emphasized her creamy curves. The sleeves were short but loose. The "lavender" dress looked old-fashioned, but not from the era she'd lived in.

Despite the lovely vision of her body and hair, her eyes were the most arresting feature of all. Sean had thought, if he ever did really see her, that she'd look like a milky-white transparent spirit—something like he'd seen in the movies. But Charlotte looked like a living, breathing woman, although he knew there was no substance to her body.

He couldn't feel her skin or clothing or hair. When he tried to wipe away her tears, nothing transferred from her skin to his. Only she could wipe away her own tears.

Not being able to do such a simple thing for Charlotte made him feel frustrated. And furious at a mother who would curse her own child. Her father certainly hadn't been a saint, and it seemed her mother wasn't much better.

Staring into her blue, blue eyes made Sean realize what he'd been denying. He liked Charlotte, really liked her. He might even have feelings for her. And now that he'd actually seen her, he knew that his attraction to her was a tangible thing. His palms were sweaty, his heart was racing, and he felt like he was a bumbling eleven-year-old boy noticing a woman for the first time.

Charlotte was ethereally beautiful in a way that he couldn't exactly describe.

"So, I can see you now."

She nodded. "You can see me now."

"But I can't touch you?"

She shrugged. It was nice to see her gestures; it added so much more to their conversation. "I am a ghost."

Sean smiled, and she smiled back. That one smile from her told him he was in trouble. He was falling in love with a woman who'd been dead for over a century.

"What happens if the curse is broken?" he had to ask.

She looked down at her hands, which she was clenching together in her lap. "It's impossible to break."

Sean placed his hand over hers. She seemed to relax, although them touching produced no sensation.

"If . . . *if* I found an apology written by my father, and *if* the owner of this house truly fell in love with me, then . . ." She lifted a single shoulder. "I suppose I would pass through to the other side, or wherever everyone else goes when they die."

Sean gazed at her, his heart tripping. "I think you might have something there. What if there was an apology written by your father? Did you ever get letters from him?"

Charlotte brought her hand to her mouth, her eyes wide. "There *were* letters. Not to me, but to my mother. I'm sure of it. She always locked them away when one came by post, and then she'd spend the next day or two isolated in her room."

"Aha!" Sean said. "I'll bet your father did apologize. How could he not? I mean, he did love your mother at some point."

"Yes, I suppose he did . . ." Charlotte said in a slow voice. She leaned forward, and Sean wished he could touch her face, her hair.

"So, where are the letters?" he asked. "Do you have them?"

Charlotte's gaze fell. "I don't know. So many things were taken from the manor over the years and sold at auctions or donated to museums. Some things might have even been destroyed." Her voice grew faint.

"We'll find them," he said, grasping her arms—well, grasping where her arms were. "We'll search the house.

And if they're not here, we'll track down collectors and put out notices."

Charlotte's gaze was on him again, hopeful.

It made Sean feel like he was actually helping her. He was pretty sure that if they could find evidence of her father's apology, then Sean could fulfill the other half of the curse.

"It's been so long," Charlotte said, as if she were testing his dedication.

"Well, I'm not going anywhere for a while," he said. He lifted one hand and ran his fingers over the hair that spilled over her shoulder. He'd never be able to touch it or truly hold her. But he could at least help her.

"Thank you," Charlotte said.

Sean's throat tightened. "Thank me when we've found those letters." He lowered his hand and rose to his feet. Then he held out his hand to Charlotte.

She smiled and placed her hand near his, then stood. He hadn't really helped her stand, but it seemed that she appreciated the gesture.

"There's no better place to start than the library, don't you agree?" Sean asked.

She was taller than he thought, but he was still looking down at her. Although the lamp in the library created a faint glow, it seemed that she had her own glow. She gazed up at him, and those blue eyes pierced right into the center of his heart.

He had a sudden urge to lean down and kiss her, but that was a foolish thought. First, he couldn't feel her, and second, he was supposed to be trying to put his life back together after his broken engagement. The breakup had only happened earlier that morning.

"I agree," she said.

He was caught off guard. What did she agree with? Then he remembered that they'd been talking about finding those letters between her parents. The letters had to be somewhere in the house, or in someone's collection. Sean was determined to help Charlotte break this damnable curse, even if his own heart broke in the process.

So, very deliberately, he stepped away from her and those blue eyes. He turned and crossed the room. "I'll start on this side," he said, gazing up at the bookcase rising above him. "Someone might have tucked them inside a book, or—"

"Or burned them," Charlotte cut in.

Sean turned. She stood in the middle of the floor, looking forlorn. He was grateful he could still see her and that she hadn't disappeared on him again. "Why would you say that?"

Charlotte blinked back tears. "I remember my mother burning letters," she said. "I don't know which ones they were, but reason stands that they were probably the ones from my father. She was angry with him until the day she died." She waved a hand toward the history book. "As you can see by her curse."

Sean folded his arms, merely to stop himself from rushing to her side. He couldn't really, truly comfort a woman he couldn't even touch. "I have another question."

Charlotte nodded, her eyes clearing a bit.

"Was your mother a witch or something?" he asked. "I mean, how else can someone cast a curse?"

She released a breath, which fascinated Sean. She heaved her shoulders as if she were actually breathing. "She wasn't a witch." Her tone was defiant.

"She was something," Sean said. "I don't know what words are appropriate for your era, but curses and ghosts aren't really a part of everyday life in the twenty-first century."

"I've found that out," Charlotte said, her tone softening. "My era was full of superstition, religious debate, plenty of doubts, and yes, soothsayers and fortunetellers. My mother said that she was a seer. I'm not sure how that translates."

Sean nodded. "Someone who could see the future?"

"Not the future," Charlotte corrected. "She had an . . . intuition about things. Good and evil. She had her routines each day that she said would ward off evil spirits. She knew all kinds of things about herbs and plants, and women in the village would pay her to be midwife to them." She crossed the room and stepped closer to Sean. "She didn't want to go on that carriage ride. But a woman was giving birth in the village, and the birth was a difficult one. The weather was stormy, and she always hated storms since she considered them a bad omen. So she asked me to come along as her 'good luck charm.'" Charlotte looked away.

"You miss her," Sean said.

Charlotte nodded and wiped at her cheek. "I miss her, but I hate her for what she did."

"I'm so sorry." He couldn't understand what the

years had been like here, roaming the manor day after day, decade after decade. But he had one more thing to ask, one more thing to say. "What if you do fulfill the curse? What if we can find those letters and there's an apology in them from your father?" He took a step closer, and she blinked her eyes up at him. Sean could very well get lost in those eyes of hers. "And what if the owner of the manor did truly fall in love with you?"

He could almost imagine he heard her heart thumping, but he knew it was his own.

Her lips parted. But before she could speak, he leaned down. He knew he couldn't kiss her, but she closed her eyes anyway as he remained motionless where their lips would have touched had she been solid.

When he lifted his head again, she opened her eyes.

"I think," she whispered. "I think I would not want to cross to the other side so quickly after all."

Sean smiled, but his heart ached. "So you would stay with the owner of the manor a little longer?"

She nodded slowly. "If I could."

He exhaled. "That's good." He moved his hand over hers, and she turned her palm up. They were palm-to-palm, but it was only a visual thing. Yet Sean felt her touch all the way to his heart.

He knew he was living in an alternate world. Everything about this situation was impossible. Any scientist or philosopher would say so. But how could Sean deny the existence of Charlotte when she was standing right in front of him, with her hand in his?

"Let's get to work, then," Sean said.

Charlotte smiled and stepped away, but not before

Sean saw the flush upon her cheeks. If she had been a living human, Sean knew he'd consider himself the luckiest person in the world.

CHAPTER 12

THEY SEARCHED WELL into the night, and by the time dawn was lighting the eastern sky, Charlotte had grown weary of the continual disappointment. They'd looked through every single, book in the library, through every desk drawer and cupboard in the house. Sean had even pulled up a loose floorboard in the Blue Room, only to find some dust.

Now they'd reached the attic. The rising sky had brightened the attic enough that Sean didn't need to turn on the light. Charlotte felt a bit possessive of the attic since it was her private domain, but Sean was respectful about asking her where he should look next.

It seemed they got along much better now that he could see her, and she caught him casting frequent glances her way. Perhaps he was still trying to convince himself that she existed. Those moments in the library had certainly been real to her, and she'd even thought she'd detected that Sean had a growing fondness for her.

Of course, the thought thrilled her yet brought dismay at the same time. She was quite fond of Sean, too, and she didn't like the thought of leaving him. Ironically, her greatest desire for centuries had been to cross over, but now . . . Now, she was hesitating.

"Have you given up already?" Sean asked, his voice a bit cross. He stood from the corner he'd been tapping to see if there was a hollow space behind it. Brushing off his hands on his pants, he focused on her.

He was tired; that was plain. Handsome still, but his hair was even more mussed, and his clothes were dirty from searching the highest and the lowest places of each room. He'd mentioned a time or two that the manor needed a good dusting. Charlotte agreed with him, but she didn't dust.

"I'm just resting," Charlotte said from her perch on the bed where she'd spent the last half hour watching Sean search. "Besides, you're new to the attic, so you'll probably think of places I would overlook."

Sean shook his head, but he wore a smile on his face.

Charlotte always felt a bit lighter when Sean smiled at her, even though she didn't weigh a single milligram.

"You seemed discouraged in the Blue Room," Sean continued, not letting her get off with a breezy answer. "You even disappeared, or dissipated, for a moment. I thought you just needed to take a break, but now you're not helping me at all."

Sean could be quite demanding.

"Maybe I'm tired."

Sean raised a brow. "Do ghosts get tired? You don't even sleep, so how could you be tired?"

Charlotte looked up at the ceiling as if she were mastering her deepest well of patience.

"I can see you when you're doing that, you know," Sean said. "You're not invisible anymore."

"Would you prefer that?" she asked, feeling annoyed now. Why did he have to be so perceptive about everything?

"No," Sean said, his voice softening. "I don't prefer you to be invisible."

He was walking toward her, and Charlotte felt a little nervous.

He stopped in front of her and settled his hands on his hips. "We're going to find it, Charlotte."

This for some reason made her feel like crying.

When she didn't respond and could only look away from him, he said, "What's wrong?"

She bit her ghostly lip. "I—I don't know. I guess that it's the case of being so close to what you've wanted for so long that you're not sure if you want it anymore."

"I get that," Sean said. "Sounds like my relationship with Michele. We always thought we knew what we wanted, or at least she did. And when it came down to it, it turned out she wanted something else entirely."

Why did he have to be so understanding?

"But I also want you to know that I'm going to keep looking for those letters," he continued. "With or without you."

It was Charlotte's turn to raise her brows. "Really?"

"Really," he said. "So you're welcome to keep watching me, or you could help. It's completely up to you."

He reached for her hand, and she lifted it as he acted as if he were pulling it toward him. And then he leaned down and kissed the top of her hand. She felt nothing from his touch, but her heart felt everything.

"Lady Charlotte," he said, one side of his mouth lifting into a smile. "I will prevail."

And somehow she knew he would. If anyone could break the curse it was Old McKinley's great-nephew.

She rose from the bed when Sean stepped back, and she started to search the books that she'd kept stacked in the bookcase. Sean continued to knock on walls and examine floorboards.

After a few moments, she said, "Someone's coming."

Sean walked to the window, and she moved behind him. A couple of moments later, a small truck pulled in at the end of the driveway.

"It's the roofer," Sean said, glancing over at her. "You have pretty good hearing."

"One of my otherworldly talents," Charlotte said with a shrug.

"Wait a minute." He turned to fully face her. "How well *can* you hear?"

She met his green gaze. "Very well."

"So you heard every conversation between Michele and me?" he asked.

"It was hard not to hear," she said. "*Neither* of you was exactly whispering."

"Could you hear me on the phone from the garden yesterday?"

It wouldn't do any good to lie. Sean could read her face too well. "Yes."

Sean fell quiet and turned his attention to the approaching truck.

"What else?" he asked.

"What else can I do that's bizarre?"

His gaze flitted toward her. "Amazing, not bizarre."

"I can smell you, too," Charlotte said. "I can't feel you, but I can feel my heart race when you're around. I don't even have a heart, so I assume it's some sort of phantom echo that my mind remembers. I can appear or disappear to people. Although I didn't try to appear in the library—my guard must have just been down, or perhaps it was my subconscious taking over."

Sean was staring at her.

She sorted through all that she'd just said. *Oh.* She'd told him her heart raced when he was around. That could be taken a few different ways, couldn't it?

Sean looked like he was about to say something, when someone started knocking on the door downstairs. Sean looked out the window again. "I should get that."

"Better you than me," she replied.

Sean didn't laugh; in fact, he looked quite serious.

She decided to stay in the attic as Sean went down the stairs and talked to the roofer. She never liked to be in the room with two people, especially if one of them could see her and the other one couldn't. It made for some awkward moments. Besides, she could hear their conversation just fine. Sean led the roofer around the house, pointing things out. When they'd agreed on the amount of repairs to be done, Sean shook the man's hand.

Then Sean returned to the manor, and Charlotte waited, listening for what he might do next. She heard him walk into the kitchen and make a phone call. He seemed to be talking to someone at a . . . library?

Charlotte hurried down the stairs, taking some liberty by skipping all of the steps. She arrived in the kitchen just as Sean hung up. He was staring at his phone.

"What did they say?" Charlotte asked.

Sean flinched, as if he hadn't heard her coming—well, of course he hadn't—or smelled her.

"They're going to search their collections and get back to me."

He was looking awfully pale for having just talked to a librarian.

"Is that all?" she asked.

"Uh, it looks like Michele called. She left a message."

Charlotte couldn't believe how deflated she felt. She knew what phone messages were—Michele had sent a voice letter through the phone. Charlotte felt like she'd gone from walking in a fragrant meadow on a sunny day to taking a sudden plunge into an icy pond. "What did Michele say?"

"I haven't listened to it yet," Sean said.

Charlotte waited.

"You'll be able to hear the message when I play it, right?" he asked.

Charlotte nodded, not sure if that was a good thing. What if Michele apologized and wanted Sean back? What if she returned to the manor? What if she interfered with Sean's help with breaking the curse?

"I guess I'd better listen to it," he said. "Maybe it's something important."

Sean pressed something on his phone, and although he put the phone up to his ear, Charlotte could hear Michele's voice coming through.

"Sean . . ." Michele started in a tentative tone. "I've really messed things up. I'm still in Scotland, and, um, I've talked to quite a few people at the pub. Turns out that everyone has a story about the ghost in the manor. So, um, you're not crazy like I accused you of. Some of these people have heard her, and one person even saw her."

Charlotte wondered who that might be. Probably Davis Farland. He'd been around a long time and used to be a pest. That is, until she appeared to him and sent him running for home. And there had possibly been a couple of others, too. Charlotte might have smiled at the memories, but everything inside her was churning at Michele's apology. How would Sean receive it? Would he call her back and tell her he wanted to reconcile?

Next, Michele laughed. "After I got out of the car and checked into the bed-and-breakfast, I slept twelve straight hours. Sleep really does wonders." She laughed again.

Charlotte was starting to hate Michele's laugh.

"Call me when you can," Michele continued. "I think we should meet. Not at the manor—I don't want to freak out again." A third laugh. Finally, she said goodbye.

Sean clicked off the recording and lowered the phone. He wasn't looking at Charlotte, which she took as a bad sign. He must be thinking of accepting Michele's apology.

Charlotte turned away. She'd get over it; she always did. She had hoped that Sean would be the one to make that difference. But he wasn't for her. And Charlotte had known that from the moment he arrived with Michele. Perhaps there was an attraction between Charlotte and Sean, but it still wasn't meant to be.

"Charlotte," Sean said in a quiet voice. She'd already walked out of the kitchen and through the foyer, and had started up the stairs.

She stopped, not sure if she wanted to hear another apology from him. But she knew that he knew she could hear him.

"I'm going to call Michele back," Sean said. "I don't want to keep her waiting."

Of course he doesn't, Charlotte thought. She hoped that Sean wouldn't hold her silence against her. If she was being realistic, she'd never see him again after this week anyway.

Charlotte couldn't get away from the sound of his voice, but she could at least go to the comfort of her attic room, where she'd be surrounded by the things that were just *hers.*

By the time she made it to the top of the stairs, she could hear Sean speaking to Michele.

Charlotte wished she could plug her ears and not hear the conversation in the kitchen below. Unfortunately, not only could she hear Sean, she could also hear Michele.

Charlotte was about to pass through the attic door when Sean said, "I've been thinking a lot about our relationship, too. And I realized that I'm grateful you broke off our engagement."

She paused on the stair landing. This wasn't what she had expected Sean to say. Where was he going with it?

"Don't you love me?" Michele said, her voice fainter than Sean's.

"I *do* love you," Sean said. "We've been dating most of our lives, it seems; how could I not? But, I'm not *in* love with you, at least not how a man who's engaged ought to be."

Michele's voice might be faint, but her emotion was clear. She was extremely upset.

"A cliché? That's what you're accusing me of? That I'm spouting clichés?" Sean asked, his voice far from soft now. "I think whatever instincts you had yesterday were correct. We shouldn't get married. Whether you want to call me crazy because of it is up to you."

Michele's reply was fast and furious, and then there was absolute silence.

It appeared that Michele had hung up.

Something slammed in the kitchen. Had Sean hit or thrown something?

Charlotte slid to the floor and sat with her back against the attic door. Even though she couldn't see Sean right now, she knew he was in pain. He might have been the one to break up with Michele, but it still couldn't have been easy.

Sean's motions in the kitchen told Charlotte that he was crossing the floor. Then the back door of the house opened and shut. He was walking outside.

Just then, the roofer started pounding right outside the attic. He was working on the roof, it seemed.

The pounding thumped through her head and into her heart. Charlotte couldn't stay up here. She went back down the stairs and out onto the patio. She could still hear the roofer pounding, but it was less intrusive now. Sean was nowhere in sight. He hadn't gone into the garden.

Charlotte looked in the direction of the barn. It wasn't her favorite place, and she couldn't go past it. It seemed there was some sort of invisible wall that kept her close to the manor. The barn was where they'd stored the broken carriage for years until it was finally burned as scrap. She knew that Old McKinley had spent plenty of time inside the barn, cleaning things out, but Charlotte also suspected that it was his way of taking a break from her. He knew that she wouldn't follow.

Was Sean in the barn? She listened closely, and above the pounding noise from the roofer, she thought she could hear movements inside the barn. Charlotte knew she could very well be imagining it.

Still, she started walking in that direction.

CHAPTER 13

SEAN SMELLED THE scent of roses before he saw Charlotte come into the barn. He should have expected her, he supposed, but he was still surprised to see her. He wasn't quite ready to rehash the conversation with Michele, and he was sure that Charlotte had heard every word he'd spoken. And possibly what Michele had replied as well.

Relationships were always complicated, but Sean had been determined to call Michele back. He'd wondered how he'd feel when he spoke to her—how his heart would feel, and what it would tell him to do. From the moment she answered the phone, he wanted to cringe. He didn't want to hear her voice; he didn't want to deal with her anymore. And it was that realization—thinking he had to "deal" with her—that had given him the answer.

He should be excited about marrying Michele. He should be looking forward to spending time with her, not cringing when she answered the phone. But had he been too cruel? What if . . . what if he *was* going crazy?

Charlotte had appeared in the barn as if she'd walked through the wall, which she probably had.

After breaking things off with Michele for a second time, he decided to expand his search for the letters. He'd scoured the house, so it made sense to look in the barn next.

But when Charlotte appeared in the barn, he realized he could see her, but she looked like a faded version of herself, as if he were looking at her through a gauze curtain.

"Charlotte, I can barely see you," Sean said, wondering if she was going to disappear altogether.

"That's because I can't go too far from the manor," she said, looking around the barn, then focusing on him. "It seems there's a limit to my ghostly ventures."

"How far can you go?" Sean asked. He'd never considered that the reason a ghost would haunt a house was because the ghost couldn't leave that house.

"About as far as the barn," she said. "On all sides."

"What happens when you try to go farther?" he asked. "I assume that you've tried to push the limits."

She nodded. "I simply can't move forward. Only backward."

"Interesting." He held up a jar of tacks he'd found on the counter that lined one of the barn walls. "Not much luck finding the letters out here."

"You're looking for the letters in the barn?" she asked, raising her faded brows. "I thought you'd be . . . pouting, or something."

"No," Sean said. "I'm definitely not pouting. Michele just helped me realize we aren't all that good together."

She nodded.

"I suppose you heard everything?" he asked.

She nodded again. "I couldn't exactly decipher all that Michele said, although she didn't sound happy."

"She wasn't."

Charlotte came closer to him, and the scent of roses grew stronger. But she was still quite transparent. "Are you all right?" she asked.

"Me?" He was surprised at the question. "It's been a long week." She was watching him closely, but it was making him nervous seeing her so transparent. It was as if the hope of breaking the curse was fading as well.

"I feel like—" she began, then looked away from him. "I feel like your breakup with Michele is my fault."

Before he could reply, she rushed on. "It's not fair that you're helping me, too." She waved a hand about the barn. "You should be meeting with a realtor, not looking for some letters that were probably burned by my mother."

"Why would she burn something that could help save you?" Sean asked.

Charlotte crossed her ghostly arms. "That's what I've been trying to figure out. Why did she curse me at all? I mean, couldn't she have cursed my father instead? Wouldn't that be more fitting and vengeful?"

"You have a point there," Sean said. There was so much he didn't understand about this strange new world he'd become involved with, and least of all how a mother's heart could be so cruel. He stepped toward Charlotte. She didn't move or back away. "I'm going to find those letters or some other form of apology. Maybe he wrote his regrets in a journal or in a letter to someone other than your mother."

"He died in Germany, Sean," Charlotte said. "We can't go to Germany and search their library archives."

He shrugged. "I could go."

Charlotte's blue eyes widened. "You can't be serious. I mean, think of the time and money it would take, and what if you didn't find anything?"

Sean's heart was thumping, and it only confirmed the choices he was making. "I have time, and I have money."

Charlotte wasn't to be dissuaded. "I thought you had a plane ticket to return to America in a few days. And what about your company?"

"I have a very able manager," Sean said. "Besides, a lot of historical documents are archived online."

"That's through the computer?"

"Yes," Sean said. "But first, I'll search the barn. I think you should go back to the house. Your transparency is making me nervous."

She stared at him for a moment. "You're not upset with me, then?"

"No," Sean said, stepping closer. "I'm not upset with you. Nothing that's happened between me and Michele is your fault. The writing was on the wall, so to speak. I just hadn't seen it until we came to Scotland. Perhaps it took leaving our tight-knit community to see that."

She was still staring at him as if she didn't believe he wasn't mad at her.

"Come on, Charlotte," Sean said stepping closer. "I'm not upset with you—if anything, I'm upset with your mother. But then again, if she hadn't cursed you, I would have never met you."

She blinked rapidly. "Do you mean it?"

He very much did mean it. Spending time in this barn had also given him a chance to think more about Charlotte without her hovering presence. He found that he'd lived through the most interesting, and even exciting, few days of his life. Ironically, he'd never felt so alive as he did when in the presence of Charlotte.

"I mean it." He didn't move; she didn't move.

Finally, she nodded, then said, "Thank you, for every-thing." She turned from him and crossed the barn, then stepped through the wall and disappeared.

Sean shoved his hands into his pockets and stood in one place for several moments. He knew he was on a wild and bizarre goose chase. One that wouldn't make sense to anyone else. He also knew that he couldn't stop, and that he had to do everything he could humanly do to find out if there was any form of written apology.

He crossed to the ladder that led to the hayloft. Maybe there was an old trunk up there with the letters. But when he reached the loft, it was bare, save for scraps of old hay. Before he went back down the ladder, another thought occurred to him.

If an apology had been written by her father in a letter or a journal, that part of the curse had already been fulfilled. Why would Charlotte have to see it with her own eyes to make it more real? That meant . . . if there was an apology out there somewhere, then they only needed the other half of the requirement to be fulfilled, and Charlotte would be on her way to the other side.

Sean's breathing grew shallow. Were they closer than they thought? Did he simply need to declare his love for her? More thoughts tumbled about his mind. Did he love her?

Yes, whispered into his mind. Although another part of his mind told him that was impossible. If he was in love with her, then how could he let her go to the other side, never to hear from her again? He leaned his head against the ladder rung, trying to sort it all out.

Sean knew he had to tell her about the fact that if her father had written an apology, or even uttered his regrets to someone, that part of the curse was already fulfilled. Would he be giving her false hope? He didn't know, but he couldn't keep her in the dark, either.

"Charlotte!" he called. Surely she could hear him, wherever she was at the moment.

He jumped the rest of the way to the barn floor and hurried to open the barn door.

"Charlotte!" he called again, running toward the manor. The country air was filled with the continual pounding of the roofer. As he pushed open the back door and was about to call out for Charlotte again, a new voice brought him up short.

"Sean! There you are!" Michele came around the corner from the kitchen.

"Michele?"

She wore a yellow sundress he hadn't seen before. He would have certainly noticed the plunging V-neck. Her dark hair was scooped into a messy bun. She wore dark red lipstick and looked as if she'd spent plenty of time on her makeup.

Inwardly, Sean groaned. He hoped this wasn't what he thought it was . . .

"I had to see you in person," Michele gushed, hurrying toward him with a plastered-on smile. "I know you've been under a lot of stress, and things in this manor are pretty bizarre." She gave a nervous laugh.

"What are you doing here?' Sean asked, taking a step back. Where was Charlotte? He couldn't smell her, but if she was in the manor, she could surely hear what was happening. He cringed, thinking that she might have her feelings hurt once again.

"I couldn't leave without seeing you," Michele said. She grasped his hand and held on tightly. "I haven't changed my plane reservations, so technically, I can stay as long as you. I . . ." She swallowed and looked about the foyer. "I could even help you. It looks like you already have a roofer working."

"Yes," Sean said, gently tugging his hand away. "Look, Michele, I meant everything I said on the phone. That hasn't changed. You were right all along. We aren't meant to be." Why was he having to go through this a third time? Weren't the first two times bad enough?

"I know what you said on the phone," Michele said, moving close again. She ran her hand up his arm and leaned into him, pressing her chest against his. "But I realized that all couples get cold feet." She moved both of her arms around his neck and raised up on her feet so that her face was level with his. "We've just had a little argument, and I forgive you, honey."

Sean practically had to peel her off him. He held her arms at her side, and she pushed her lips into a pout.

"It was a breakup, Michele," he said. "Now, I've got a million things to do. So I'd appreciate it if you could leave now."

Michele didn't seem fazed at all. She leaned toward him again, and this time, she tugged his shirt toward her. "Come on, sweetie. You can't possibly be choosing a ghost over me. I'm all real, Sean. *All real.*"

Her other hand slid around his waist.

"Michele," Sean ground out. "Please let go of me." He'd never been so angry at a person in his entire life. Michele had pushed him to his limit. And then he smelled roses. He knew that Charlotte was somewhere in the room, watching Michele paw him.

"Charlotte," he said. "Can you help me?"

Michele drew away at that. "You're still talking to her? She's a freaking ghost, Sean! That means she's *dead*!"

Sean leveled his gaze at Michele and her flushed face. "She might be dead, but she can hear everything you're saying and see everything you're doing." He looked past Michele. Why couldn't he see Charlotte? She had to be there; he could smell her.

"Can you help me, Charlotte?" he repeated.

Michele took another step back, raising her hands. "What are you doing, Sean?" Her voice rose with each word. "What are you asking her to do? Call her off!"

Sean shoved his hands in his pockets. He had no doubt that Charlotte would be happy to help him scare off Michele, and he also knew that Charlotte couldn't really hurt anyone. He supposed he should feel a little guilty about what was about to happen. Even if he didn't know exactly what that might be.

First, the front door clicked open. Michele turned her head to look, and Sean saw that no one was standing on the other side.

"Is that her?" Michele asked.

Sean didn't have time to answer because suddenly Michele gasped and nearly staggered to the floor.

Sean reached out a hand to stop her from falling, but Michele righted herself, and without another word, she hurried outside, nearly tripping down the stairs in her haste.

Sean just stared at Michele as she yanked open the door of the car she'd arrived in, jumped in, and sped off down the drive. He leaned against the doorway, wondering exactly what Charlotte had done to Michele and whether or not he should feel guilty about it.

Michele turned at the top of the drive and continued onto the main road. Sean had the feeling that she wouldn't be returning this time.

"What does it feel like?" he asked when he smelled roses.

Charlotte didn't answer for a moment, and Sean hoped he hadn't breached some ghost code of ethics by asking.

Finally, she said, "I don't know. I think it's maybe like being dashed with cold water."

"What does it feel like to *you*?" Sean asked.

Another pause. "The best way to explain it would be having my breath taken away for a moment."

Sean turned to look back at the foyer. "Why can't I see you?"

Her form took shape in front of him. The sunlight

coming in from the front door made her seem to glow. To Sean's relief, she was much more solid looking than she'd been in the barn.

Her red hair tumbled like wisps about her shoulders, and her bright blue eyes were full of mischief, focused on him.

"That's better," he said, coming into the foyer. "Can you show me?"

Her eyebrows lifted. "You want me to walk through you?"

"Is that what you did to Michele and the airport driver?"

A smile curved her lips. "Yes."

"Then . . ." Sean smiled. "Walk through me, too. I want to know how it feels."

CHAPTER 14

CHARLOTTE OPENED HER mouth, then closed it. She stood in the foyer, facing Sean, and he'd just asked her to walk through him. This was her best trick—the one that was guaranteed to send a patron of the manor running, spooked beyond reason. "No, I don't think so," she told Sean, even though it was hard to resist the way his green eyes were imploring her. "As you've witnessed twice now, it's not a pleasant experience for humans."

Sean tilted his head and studied her. She really wanted to touch his hair, his cheek, his shoulder. "Maybe because they weren't expecting it," Sean said in that low voice of his. The voice that made her feel more human than she'd felt in centuries.

"I don't want to hurt you," she said at last.

Sean smiled then, and Charlotte knew that she'd lost her heart to him. For a while now. Watching him resist Michele and then call upon her for help had only endeared him more to her. Charlotte could very well understand why Michele was so upset about their breakup.

After shutting the door behind him, Sean walked closer to Charlotte. This made the foyer feel smaller and more intimate. The pounding on the roof had temporarily stopped, so the silence between them was palpable.

"You won't hurt me," Sean said. "I'll be expecting it. You don't have to worry about me screaming and running out the front door."

Charlotte had to tilt her head up to meet his gaze. His expression was one of earnestness, as well as amusement. "I don't think so," she said at last. No matter how tempting it might be to walk through Sean, to feel what it might be like to be completely surrounded by his body, she'd seen the look of horror in the eyes of the people she'd invaded. She didn't want that to happen between her and Sean.

"Charlotte," he said, his hand moving to her shoulder.

She couldn't feel his touch, but she could feel his gesture reaching her heart, which didn't seem quite so dead after all. She didn't speak for a moment, then she said, "All right. You might want to brace yourself, though."

Sean nodded and leaned his other hand against the wall next to them.

"You have a lot of confidence in yourself," she observed.

He gave her a wink. "I'm ready."

Charlotte inched closer until they were standing chest to chest. She could hear the thump of his heart and the intonations of his breathing. Sean kept his eyes open, looking down at her, but Charlotte felt she had to close her eyes for some reason. She took a half step forward.

Sean inhaled sharply, but he didn't move. Charlotte could hear his heart racing—it was like she was using a doctor's stethoscope to listen to his drumming pulse. She felt . . . light, yet heavy at the same time. It was as if Sean's body were giving her more sustenance.

She stepped back, putting space between them. She looked up at him, feeling a bit unsteady herself.

Sean had closed his eyes, and now he exhaled slowly. His expression was relaxed, though, not pained like she thought it might be. She didn't dare speak, not until she knew he was all right.

When he opened his eyes, they were green and clear. He leaned down and whispered, "I want to kiss you."

Charlotte felt a rush of warmth flood her. "You can't."

Still, he stayed close to her, searching her eyes. She wondered if she'd be able to cross to the other side knowing that she wouldn't see him again.

"I need to tell you something," he said.

Charlotte's ghostly heart tripped. "Yes?"

He told her his theory about her father's apology. How even if her father was dead, whenever or wherever he apologized, it would still be valid. "So you see," he continued. "If an apology was made, either in writing or verbally, then that part of the requirement has already been fulfilled. The trouble is, we don't know whether or not that's the case."

The foyer was extremely warm, Charlotte realized.

All this contact with Sean seemed to make her feel a little more human than usual.

"It could take years to find out," Charlotte said. "If it's even accessible."

"I'd like to assume that your father did apologize at one point, to someone, and perhaps even to your mother in a letter."

Charlotte wanted to believe that, too. "So, now what?"

"That, dear Charlotte, is up to you," Sean said. He turned slightly and leaned against the wall, watching her.

"How so?" she asked, although she thought she knew what he was talking about. Did she want Sean to profess that he cared about her? And then did she want to fade away from this earthly existence? Never to see him again?

"What if I told you that I was in love with you?" he said.

Charlotte couldn't look at him. Tears started to fall down her cheeks. "Then ... then I suppose the curse would be broken."

"Charlotte," he said. "Look at me."

She blinked away the tears and looked at Sean. He'd straightened from the wall and was holding out his hand. She felt shaky and unsteady, but she reached toward him and placed her hand on top of his open palm. "I—I don't want to leave anymore," she said. "But I know you have a life outside of this manor, and I can't expect you to stay here with me."

"You need to let me decide that," Sean said, moving closer.

"I've already decided," Charlotte said. "You might

say you care for me, but I can't let you live here, trapped like me." She stepped back, then she turned and glided up the stairs until she reached the attic. The pounding on the roof started up again, only adding to her consternation.

She made sure the attic door was locked before she settled on her bed and let the tears fall. Sean had to leave the manor. He had to live his life, without her. No matter what happened, and no matter how convincing Sean might be, she couldn't open the attic door and let him in any longer.

She stayed there the rest of the day, half hoping, half expecting Sean to come up to the attic. But he didn't.

When the sun set, the pounding on the roof finally stopped. She heard the roofer drive away, and not too long after, she heard Sean leave the house.

Tempted as she was, she stayed on her bed and didn't look out the window. A car started, and she knew it was his. She stayed on her bed as the sun sank out of sight and twilight spread across the fields surrounding the manor.

Charlotte stayed in the attic for two days—two whole days of no sound in the manor. Sean hadn't returned, and neither had the roofer.

So when Charlotte heard the sound of a car coming up the drive, she leapt from her bed and crossed to the window. Sean was back. She didn't move as she watched him climb out of the car and shut the door. Questions about where he'd been, what he'd been doing, and if he was ever coming back had plagued her mind.

But now that he was back, she didn't want to see him. She didn't want to face the fact that she could never truly be with him. They lived in two different worlds that could never be reconciled.

She stepped back from the window just as he looked up toward the attic.

"Charlotte," he said, not loudly at all. It was as if he knew she was there, watching him.

Don't answer, she told herself, clenching her hands into fists. She crossed the room and sat on her bed again, wondering how many more days until he returned to America. How many more days of his presence could she endure?

She heard him come up the stairs, his footsteps sure and steady.

Sean didn't knock on the door, and he didn't call out to her.

He sat down on the floor, casting a shadow under the door. It sounded like he was shuffling some papers.

"I've had an interesting two days," he said as if she were sitting right next to him. "I spoke to Davis Farland and his wife. They told me about all of the legends surrounding your curse over the centuries."

Charlotte leapt from the bed, raced across the room, and slid through the door. "What did they say?"

Sean grinned up at her. "Thought you might appear when you heard that."

Charlotte narrowed her eyes. "Are you tricking me?"

"Never," he said in a perfectly serious voice, although his gaze was still full of amusement. "Sit by me." He patted the floor beside him.

"It's not ladylike to sit on the floor," she said.

Sean patted the floor again.

"Oh, all right," she huffed, and sat next to him, carefully arranging her dress about her legs.

"Farland told me that a curse can only be broken in a formal setting," he said.

"What does he mean by that?" Charlotte asked. It was strange and wonderful to be sitting next to Sean as if they were two completely normal, living people.

"He said that it was more likely to be broken on the anniversary of the curse," Sean continued. "Which, according to him, is tomorrow."

"Tomorrow?" Charlotte kept track of years and seasons, but never dates. No, dates were too depressing to watch tick by.

"Tomorrow," Sean restated, leaning closer. He lowered his voice. "Are you ready, Charlotte?"

She felt fluttery all over, and she knew it wasn't because of the possibility of the curse finally being broken. It was because of Sean's nearness. Did his green eyes have to be so green and his skin so healthy and golden?

"What about my father's apology?" she asked.

Sean held up a sheet of paper that was folded over a couple of times. "The library called me back, and the archivist found something. Your father made a public apology, and it was published about fifty years later in the village's weekly paper."

Charlotte couldn't grasp the page, but Sean opened up the folded paper.

"What does it say, and how did I not know about it?" she asked.

"Look at this," Sean said. "This article was written by T. Elliott Meyer about fifty years after your father's death.

He'd been doing research on the village and uncovered the legend of the curse. So he dug up records and testimonials from villagers. He interviewed one woman, who was a cook at the manor, who said that your father came to the manor one night about two years after you and your mother's death. He seemed to be in a terrible temper. He was rude and demanding to the staff, and then he went into your mother's old room and said some things that the cook said she'd never forget."

Charlotte stared at the newspaper writing, stunned. "What . . . what does it say?" She couldn't bring herself to read Meyer's article herself.

Sean stared to read:

"Mrs. Channing overheard King Ernest II's strange soliloquy at the gravesite of his deceased lover. Ernest II said, 'Haven't I given you enough, Constance? You know that my position wouldn't allow me to make you my wife. I've apologized often enough for that, but now you have created a farce out of my good name. Accept my apology, once and for all. Nothing grieves me more than to think I've done you and our daughter wrong.' Mrs. Channing said he continued to repeat himself over and over, and finally, he left the graveyard, riding horseback as if he were being chased by the devil himself."

Charlotte stared at the words that seemed to blur before her eyes. Could it be true? Had her father been to the graveyard, speaking to her dead mother's spirit, imploring her to forgive him? Charlotte would have no way of knowing if her father had showed up at the graveyard; it was too far for her spirit to travel.

Now, she read it again, on her own. Sean watched her reaction, and finally she looked up at him in awe. "You spent two days finding this, for *me*?"

Sean nodded, and Charlotte didn't know if it was such a good idea sitting this close to him. Letting him tell her things that might finally set her free. Getting her hopes up . . . Because, when it came down to it, and if the curse really was broken, she'd be giving up Sean.

"What will happen to us?" she couldn't help but ask.

Sean gave her a half smile. "I don't know. But I suppose we need to prepare for accepting whatever does."

"All right," she said, exhaling. This was what she'd wanted for centuries. She just had to prepare herself. "Tomorrow, then."

"Tomorrow," Sean echoed, still watching her.

Then, ever so slowly, she leaned her head against his shoulder. She wasn't really resting her head, because there was no weight to rest. But she wanted to feel human, if only for a short time.

CHAPTER 15

SEAN PACED THE kitchen. He had everything in place, ready to break the curse—everything that he'd found online and that Davis Farland had suggested. Sean had lit several candles and placed them about the room, keeping all electricity off. Farland had suggested making things as close to the nineteenth century as possible. So Sean had hidden away any modern appliances in the cupboards. He'd covered up the stove and oven with a large burlap sack. He'd carried out the chairs and brought in a couple of the Victorian-era pieces. Upon the table was an antique box he'd found in the library, and inside he put a few things that he'd be using in the ceremony.

Someone walking into the kitchen would have thought Sean had created a nineteenth-century film set. Outside, even the weather was cooperating. The wind had started up, and dark clouds had moved in.

Charlotte had told him the carriage accident had happened on a stormy Friday night, and she and her mother had suffered a long, painful decline and had finally expired on Saturday evening. She guessed around eight p.m. based on everything she'd ever read or heard.

It was nearly eight o'clock now, and still Charlotte hadn't appeared. Sean was getting nervous. Rain pattered against the windows, sending a chill through him. What if something went wrong? What if this didn't work at all? He knew she had feelings for him, and he'd already told her he was falling in love with her. What if she decided to botch all of this? Avoid him until the window of time had passed them by?

Then he smelled roses.

"Charlotte?" he said, turning toward the foyer.

She entered the kitchen, and Sean could only describe her as breathtaking. She'd pulled her hair back into a sort of twisted braid. She'd somehow tucked small rosebuds into her hair. Tendrils of red curled along her face, and her eyes seemed a brighter blue than usual.

Her "lavender" dress hugged her curves, then flowed against her legs. She was barefoot, and her cheeks were flushed.

"You came," he said. She was there, but she didn't look entirely happy. Shouldn't she be ecstatic that she could finally cross over?

Sean gestured to the chair at the head of the table. "For the lady of the manor."

She nodded regally and swept into the chair, sitting straight with her chin lifted. But her eyes didn't meet his.

"Charlotte," Sean said. "You can look at me."

She blinked, then looked up at him. "Sorry."

He crouched before her and placed his hand where hers rested on her lap. "Are you ready?"

Her eyes were moist, but her gaze remained steady. She lifted her chin another notch. "I am."

Sean cleared his throat and sat in the chair closest to where Charlotte was sitting. He'd memorized the words that he was about to say—according to the ancient reverse curses he'd studied—and he hoped that he would do it right the first time. The wind outside had picked up, and the rain intensified. It only created a more intimate atmosphere accented by the glow of candlelight.

"Charlotte," he began. "Upon your mother's death, she cursed you with remaining in this world until two events happened." He reached into the antique box. "This article that quotes your father's apology releases you from the first part of your curse."

Charlotte reached out to touch the paper, and Sean noticed the trembling of her hand. She nodded and folded her hands back on her lap, keeping her gaze on Sean.

"Your father treated you and your mother like you were second-class and sent you to this manor to live out your days, away from his royal life," Sean said. "But his apology has been accepted, and he can now be forgiven of his wrongdoings during his life."

A few of the candles flickered, and the light in the room momentarily dimmed. Sean felt a little spooked, but he plowed on, repeating the words he'd practiced in his mind.

"A second condition has to be fulfilled in order to completely break the curse," Sean said. He reached for the rose he'd placed in the antique box and picked it up. It was a dark pink, reminding him of the flush of Charlotte's cheeks when she'd first come into the kitchen.

He turned toward her again. "Charlotte," he said, trying to keep his voice steady although the wind and rain were now pelting the windows as if trying to break them. More candles flickered, and a few of them went completely out, leaving behind only thin trails of white smoke.

Sean moved off the chair and knelt on one knee.

Charlotte's eyes widened, and she brought a hand to her mouth.

"When I first saw your portrait hanging at the base of the stairs, I was mesmerized," he said. "But when I heard your voice, I was entranced."

"Sean," Charlotte whispered, looking worried.

Wasn't she supposed to be hanging on every word he said?

"I think I started falling in love with you that time we spent all night talking," Sean said. "I've never met anyone like you, ghost or human, and I'd like you to take this rose as a token of my love."

The wind died down all at once, and the rain stopped. Even the candles seemed to stop flickering. The room was absolutely silent.

Charlotte reached toward the rose, and Sean watched as her fingers wrapped around the stem. She couldn't grasp it, so Sean kept it where her hand had curled around it.

Her eyes met his, and a single tear dripped down her cheek. Sean reached up with his other hand to touch the tear, although he knew he couldn't actually wipe it away.

"Sean," she whispered in a faint voice.

And that's when Sean realized she was becoming more and more transparent, like she had in the barn. Panic jolted through him, and he wanted to tell her not to disappear. But he didn't think she had control over what was happening, because the dismay on her face made his stomach feel like it had been hollowed out.

"Sean," she mouthed, but no sound came out.

"Charlotte!" Sean said. "Don't . . ." He had to let her go. "Goodbye," he said instead. "I love you."

The final candle flickered out, and the sounds of wind and rain returned.

Sean sat there in the dark, completely alone, as the storm swirled outside.

Charlotte was gone. Not only had he seen her fade from his eyes, but he felt her absence from the manor, from this room, as if something tangible had gone missing. The manor felt different. Forlorn, somehow.

Sean rested his elbows on the table and dropped his head into his hands. The scent of roses was gone. The rose he'd picked from the garden had faded with Charlotte. All he could smell was melted candle wax.

CHAPTER 16

CHARLOTTE FELT AS if she were floating, but it wasn't of her own accord or power. She couldn't see anything, although it wasn't dark, nor light. But she was surrounded by sounds—sounds of life, of voices, or breathing, of hearts beating.

"Hello?" she said, testing out her voice. It was a whisper, but audible, at least to her ears. Charlotte had a feeling that no one could hear her. "Where am I?" she said aloud.

No one answered, yet she could hear several voices speaking. Not to one another, but speaking all the same. Someone was quoting poetry. Someone laughed.

Then a voice became distinguishable above the others, a voice she hadn't heard in over a century.

"Mother?" Charlotte said.

The voices continued, ebbing and flowing, sometimes muted, sometimes clear.

"Charlotte?" her mother returned.

Charlotte felt a warmth begin in her heart and spread

to the rest of her limbs—limbs she knew weren't there, but it felt like she was more human than she'd been in death.

"Where are you, Mother?" Charlotte said, looking around. There were no shapes of dark or light that she could make out.

"You've crossed over?" her mother said.

Had she? And if so, wouldn't her mother know? "I think so," Charlotte said. "Unless I'm dreaming."

"The dead don't dream," her mother said in a light voice. Her voice was more distinct now, closer than it had been. The other voices seemed to fade away.

"Why can't I see you?" Charlotte continued. "And where am I? Where are you?"

"You're in the void," her mother said. "It seems the curse was broken, but you haven't accepted it yet."

"I don't understand," Charlotte said.

Her mother gave a soft laugh, and this time it sounded as if she were standing, or floating, right next to Charlotte. Charlotte reached out a hand but felt nothing in front of her.

"When you reach the void, you're given a choice," her mother said. "You can accept or reject your judgment."

Charlotte was intrigued, but confused. "How does that work?"

"I don't know," her mother said. "Everyone accepts their judgment." She paused. "Except for you, it seems."

"I've been dead for centuries," Charlotte said. "The curse is broken. What more do I have to do to cross over?"

"About the curse ..." Her mother released a sigh.

"It's frowned upon over here. It seems that I took liberties where I had no right."

"But the curse held fast," Charlotte said.

"Yes, unfortunately," her mother said. "I have asked for redemption."

Another voice that had faded now grew louder, although Charlotte couldn't make out the exact words of the person speaking.

Her mother's presence seemed to grow weaker. Then she spoke again. "It seems that you do have a choice, Charlotte." The second voice faded, and her mother's presence grew closer.

"A choice about what?" Charlotte asked.

"As part of my redemption, you can choose to finish living out your life," her mother said. "Or you can cross over. It is up to you."

Charlotte wished she could see her mother, wished she could see her surroundings. She didn't know what was real or what she might be imagining. "If I finish living out my life, do I go back to the date of my death?"

"I don't know, daughter," her mother said. "I don't know."

Charlotte let the information settle in. The voices that had faded earlier now seemed to surround her. The poetry reader was back, reciting something she wasn't familiar with. The man's voice reminded her of Old McKinley. He'd liked poetry. Had he ever recited it aloud?

Charlotte thought of the last moments with Sean. How he'd given her a rose cut from her own garden. How he'd disappeared for two days to find out if the curse could be broken. How his last words had been "I love you."

"Do you forgive me, Charlotte?" her mother's voice rose above the rest for a brief moment.

Charlotte had spent decades as a victim of her mother's curse. But it all seemed only a small moment now. "I forgive you."

"Then make your choice, daughter."

If she chose to live out the rest of her life, what did that mean? Where would she live, and what century would she be in? Charlotte exhaled, releasing a long breath. And it was a breath. A breath she didn't know she had.

"I choose to live," she whispered.

She imagined her mother smiling. Those blue eyes that she'd inherited sparkling with amusement and approval. Then the bubble of warmth faded, replaced by a sharp stinging on her left side. Coldness spread across her skin, and wet seeped into her clothing. She was wet.

Charlotte dragged her eyes open to see darkness in various shades. Above her was a tree, and beyond that, faint stars glimmered in the night sky. Was she in the garden? Her eyes felt dry and gritty, and there was a strange taste in her mouth.

About the time she realized she could taste, she realized she could breathe. And . . . her pulse was racing. Charlotte tried to sit up, but her body didn't obey—at least not in the way she expected it to. Her stomach contracted, and her neck strained.

Charlotte stretched out her fingers. Beneath them was . . . dirt.

She gasped. Was she . . . human? Slowly, she lifted

her hand until she'd moved it in front of her face. Bits of dirt had smeared across her skin.

Charlotte's chest tightened, and her throat felt like it was on fire with the pressure of a swelling sob. She turned over onto her side and stared at the rough bark of a tree trunk. Reaching out, she touched the trunk. It was rough and cool. She could feel the trunk! Her hand was not going through the bark.

"I'm alive," she whispered.

She turned her head to scan the area, guessing it was still a couple of hours before dawn would arrive. Bracing both hands on the ground, she pushed herself to a sitting position. She was not in the garden. The road was rutted, but familiar. This was the spot where the carriage had wrecked. This was the place where her life had started to end.

Charlotte drew her knees to her chest and realized her lavender dress was torn and tattered, as if she'd run through a thicket of brambles. She had dirt smeared on her legs, and her feet were bare. She lifted a hand to check her hair. It had come undone and tangled wildly about her head and shoulders.

But she could feel each strand and each tangle. She ran her hands down the sides of her face, along her neck, over her chest. She stopped over her beating heart and took several breaths. She was really, truly alive.

"Sean," she whispered. Had she lost him after all? Was she in the past, waiting for a carriage driver to come by and see her?

Charlotte clutched her knees to her chest and rested her chin on the tops of them. She hadn't meant to cry, but the tears came fast and hot. Perhaps she was dreaming, or perhaps this was all real, and she truly was alive.

For now, she'd simply be. Was it better to not know which year it was? If she delayed, then she could still dream. The air stirred around her, a soft breeze with a hint of coolness but a promise of warmth. The scents of moist earth, new grass, and fresh leaves told Charlotte that it was late spring.

As the eastern sky lightened and the sun finally spilled over the distant hills, the dew on the ground sparkled in the early brightness.

Charlotte's body seemed to be humming with life and energy and wonder. And . . . her stomach felt hollow. She was hungry. She laughed then. How glorious to feel hunger. With the lightening landscape, she took courage and rose to her unsteady feet. The ground was rough and cool beneath them. Small rocks pricked at her delicate skin as she took her first few steps.

She had not forgotten how to walk, and for that, she breathed easier. But where to walk?

Charlotte scanned the terrain. The rutted road ran a couple hundred meters, then melded into a wild growth of tall grasses. It seemed this road was not regularly used. Did that mean . . . ? Hope was hammering its way through Charlotte, but she suppressed it.

She started to walk in the direction of what she thought was the manor. She had no idea what condition she'd find it in. Perhaps she'd arrived in the future and the manor wouldn't be there at all. Or perhaps she'd arrived soon after her earthly death and would give everyone a frightful scare.

Her steps slowed as she wondered what might happen to her without the parentage of her mother. Would she have to become a servant? Perhaps she could be a governess, for she'd been well educated in the nineteenth century.

Charlotte climbed a short hill, and at the top, she saw the village spread before her. At first her heart sank because smoke rose from several places, indicating that people were cooking at their hearths. Then she realized the smoke was coming from a couple of fields. Farmers were burning winter rot.

And then her heart skipped a couple of beats. On the far side of the village, a car was driving along a road. A car! It was at least the latter half of the twentieth century. She watched the car, wishing it were closer. She'd seen the various eras of motor vehicles, of course, and this car looked quite modern.

Could it be?

Next her gaze traveled to the hill that rose just before the manor. Charlotte knew that once she reached that hill, she'd be able to see the manor. She started toward it, at first walking and picking her way through the grass and rocks, then running. She didn't care about her feet getting scraped on the ground and her thighs burning from the exertion. Charlotte had to see the manor.

As she crested the hill, she slowed.

The manor looked mostly the same. In fact, it looked as if some upgrades had been made. She could see the rose bushes behind the house had been recently pruned. The barn had been painted. And the car parked in front of the manor . . . was not Sean's.

Her heart sank. She didn't recognize the car, which might not mean much, but she knew it didn't belong to any of the manor owners that she'd known.

Charlotte continued down the hillside, her heart pounding, her head feeling light with the warming sun, her stomach empty and tight.

She was thirsty and hungry at the same time, but a deep despair was also growing within her. Where had Sean gone? What year was it? How would she survive in this modern world?

She reached the side of the barn. The closer she got, the more changes she saw. Someone had planted a vegetable garden. She heard the nicker of a horse coming from inside the barn. New trees had been planted, lining the driveway and extending to the main road. Two large planters brimming with red and white flowers sat on either side of the front door to the manor.

And then she heard a female voice.

"Sean! Can you come downstairs?"

Sean was here. But another woman was here as well. Was it Michele? Had they reconciled?

Charlotte wavered. She didn't want Sean to see her like this. She didn't want to come face-to-face with Michele. Everything inside of her seemed to freeze, and then she felt too hot. What was happening to her?

Her vision darkened, and just as she collapsed, she wondered if her life had just ended for a second time.

CHAPTER 17

SEAN KNEW HE shouldn't be impatient with his sister, but Eloise had overstayed her welcome in Scotland as far as he was concerned. So what if he'd sold his construction company and turned into a hermit living in a remote village in Scotland, pining after a woman who he'd never actually touched and who had disappeared from his kitchen almost two years ago?

Yes, two years. Sean could hardly believe that the fateful night had been so long ago. Sometimes it seemed as if it had all happened yesterday; other times, it felt as if it had never happened.

At least that's what Eloise had been trying to talk to him about. It hadn't helped that Michele had ratted him out when she finally returned to America. Sean and Eloise had had a few conversations on the phone, and he'd been able to convince her he was completely fine.

For the most part, Eloise had believed him. Until she graduated from law school and passed the bar. Apparently she'd been given a job at an upscale Denver law firm, but she'd asked for a two-week delayed start date. With her advance and her free time, she'd purchased a plane ticket to Scotland.

And here she was. Calling him downstairs. Again. He'd told her more than once not to bother cooking for him. He was a well-established bachelor now and preferred his own routine. With Eloise's visit, he'd given her the master bedroom on the main floor, and he'd taken up residence in Charlotte's attic room. It was quite cozy, although it kept the painful memories more alive than usual.

He thought he'd been pretty good at hiding it all until the night before, when Eloise had discovered his stash of books on subjects such as time travel, life after death, occult mysteries . . . just to name a few.

Sean now considered himself not only the village's resident handyman, but also an expert on all things supernatural and spiritual. He was just missing his wizard robes—at least that's what Eloise had accused him of during their colossal argument.

Frankly, he was surprised she was speaking to him this morning. And so early.

But her voice when she'd said, "Sean! Can you come downstairs?" wasn't her normal tone. In fact, it sounded a bit panicked.

So, he'd set aside Old McKinley's diary—which Sean liked to read on the occasional morning in case he could glean any fresh insights into Charlotte's curse and what might have happened to her—and opened the attic door.

He trudged down the stairs to find Eloise standing at the wide-open front door.

"What's going on?" he asked.

"Look," she said, her voice much softer now and holding a hint of fear.

Sean joined her at the doorway. Something was in their driveway. It was a . . . person. "What the hell?"

"It's a woman," Eloise said in a fierce whisper. "I saw her walking toward the house. That's when I called. Her clothing is filthy, and she was walking like she was drunk or something. What if she's one of those addicts who tries to hide in people's houses and steal their food and money?"

"What are you talking about?" Sean asked, staring at the form. It was a woman, all right. Her arms and legs were bare. Her dress was faded blue, or light purple; it was hard to tell from where he was standing.

"I saw a report on the news last week," Eloise continued. "Remember I told you? These vagrants squat in country homes and barns, living weeks at a time unde-tected."

Sean was hardly paying attention to what his sister was prattling on about. He crossed the threshold and started down the stairs.

"Sean!" Eloise called after him. "She could be playing dead. Maybe she's going to attack us. Sean! We should call the police first!"

"She needs a doctor, not the police," Sean shot back, breaking into a jog. The woman's auburn hair was tangled and covering most of her face and neck. As he neared, his heart leapt into his throat.

This woman . . . she looked like . . .

Charlotte.

Sean knelt next to her and pressed his fingers against her throat. "She's breathing," he said to himself. Eloise was still on the porch, yelling out inane warnings.

Sean's eyes stung with tears, and his throat tightened so much he had trouble catching his breath. "You're . . . you're alive." His head was spinning, and he felt as if he'd walked off a roller coaster.

"Charlotte? What's happened to you? How did you get here?" he said, his words tumbling out so fast. He blinked against the burning in his eyes, then ever so carefully, he scooped her up in his arms.

Roses.

She still smelled like roses.

What had happened to her? She had scrapes on her arms and hands and feet but didn't appear otherwise injured. And she was breathing. That was the most important thing. Her weight in his arms was another wonder—that he could touch her, feel her, carry her.

"I'm calling the police," Eloise said as he neared the porch. "And don't you dare bring that woman into the house. Who knows what kind of diseases she's carrying?"

"Eloise!" Sean barked at his sister. "Shut up."

Eloise's eyes widened, and her mouth fell open.

"This is Charlotte," he said, pushing past his stunned sister. "She's come back to me."

Eloise followed him into the master bedroom. "What did you say?"

Sean set her down on the bed. He didn't care if dirt got onto the bedspread. Without answering Eloise, he leaned over Charlotte and smoothed her tangled hair from her face. Her eyes were still closed, but he'd know her anywhere. In the flesh, she was even more beautiful. Her long eyelashes lay against her smudged cheeks, and her lips were pink against her pale skin.

Too pale.

Eloise was still hovering, and at least she'd stopped making threats to call the police. She walked around the bed and sat on the other side from Sean. "It's really her?"

Sean nodded.

"How?" Eloise started. "How is this possible?"

He rubbed at his face, staring down at Charlotte. "I don't know. I haven't been able to find the answers in any books."

Eloise nodded, subdued. Then after a moment of them both staring at Charlotte in wonder, Eloise said, "Should we call the ambulance?"

"I don't know," Sean said. He took Charlotte's hand in his, pressing his fingers against her wrist. "Her pulse is strong and steady. It's like she's just sleeping."

Just then, Charlotte's eyes opened.

Sean nearly dropped her hand in surprise, but her fingers tightened around his.

"Sean?" she said. Her voice was faint, but Sean knew it well. "Is it really you? Are you really here?"

"Yes," he said, feeling a laugh push through his chest. His heart was galloping. "It's really me."

She blinked those blue eyes—blue eyes that Sean had dreamed about every night for the past two years. Then she turned her head toward Eloise.

"Hello," Eloise said in a faint voice.

When Sean saw the crease of Charlotte's brow, he was quick to say, "This is Eloise, my sister."

Charlotte's face seemed to relax, and she looked back at Sean. They didn't say anything for a long moment. Sean wasn't sure what to ask first.

"Well," Eloise finally said, clearing her throat. "I'll go get you something to drink."

"I'm so hungry," Charlotte blurted out, then her beautiful pale skin flushed pink.

Eloise smiled. "Very well. I'll be back shortly with something to eat as well."

When Eloise left the room, she shut the door behind her, which Sean thought very tactful of her.

He brought Charlotte's hand to his lips and kissed the back of it. "What in the world happened to you?"

A soft smile lit her face. "I can't believe it's you—that you're here. I—I didn't know what year it was, or if I'd gone back or forward in time."

Sean studied her. "How much time do you think has passed?"

"A few hours?" she said. "It—it was sort of like a dream. I spoke to my mother, and she told me I had a choice to make. Then I opened my eyes, and I was in a field not far from here. I was so afraid that you'd be gone. That I'd missed you."

Sean linked his fingers through hers. "The last time I saw you, in the kitchen, was two years ago."

Her eyes widened, and she bit her lip. "Two years?"

Sean nodded.

"And you're still here?"

Eloise opened the door. "He's still here," she said in an affectionate voice.

This was certainly a different sister than the previous night, Sean decided.

Eloise came into the room, carrying a cup of hot tea and a small plate of biscuits. "Here, try this." She handed over the tea to Sean while she helped Charlotte sit up in the bed. Eloise was quick to situate another pillow behind her.

Sean quite liked this side of his sister.

Charlotte took a sip of the tea and released a satisfied sigh. "Much better."

"Good to hear." Eloise folded her arms and smiled. "Because Sean, my brother here, sold his company after you ... disappeared. He decided to stay in Scotland permanently." She met Sean's gaze, approval in her eyes, which surprised him. "Apparently," Eloise continued, "he had a lot more faith in your return than I did."

"You ..." Charlotte set down the teacup on the bedside table, then met Sean's gaze. "You've been here for two years. *Waiting for me?*"

Sean smiled, his heart feeling like it might leap out of his chest. He shrugged, trying to act nonchalant. "The manor grew on me."

Eloise stepped away from the bed. "I'll just be in the kitchen, if either of you need something."

Neither of them said anything until Eloise left the room and shut the door again.

"Sean," Charlotte whispered. "Am I dreaming?" She lifted her other hand and traced his cheek and jaw with her fingers.

And suddenly they were in each other's arms. Sean couldn't believe she was living, breathing, full of substance. Her hair smelled of roses and fresh earth.

"I'm so dirty," she said with a half laugh and pulled him closer.

The warmth of her breath on his neck and the feel of her soft body against his own was making it hard for Sean to let her go.

"I'm sorry that you had to wait two years," she whispered.

Sean closed his eyes, memorizing the feel of her in his arms. "I'm sorry, too," he said. "And I'm glad it wasn't any longer."

She drew away, but only by a short distance. "Can you kiss me now?"

Sean didn't need to be asked twice, and he lowered his mouth to hers. She responded instantly, as if she'd been imagining this moment as long as he had. Her mouth was soft and warm beneath his, and as their kiss deepened, her hold tightened. His body was responding in ways that might make things awkward if Eloise were to come back into the room.

Thankfully, his sister had the good sense to stay out.

"Sean," Charlotte said, breaking off the kiss and running her hands over his shoulders. "I can't believe you're real, that *this* is real."

"Do you want to pinch me?" he asked with a grin.

Charlotte laughed. "No." She tugged him hard, pulling him down.

Sean rolled onto the bed and pulled her against him, until their bodies were flush, their legs intertwined. He kissed her long and slow, taking his time, never wanting the kiss to end.

"I really need a bath," she murmured against his mouth.

"Later," he said, running his hand across her back, then dipping his head to kiss the soft skin of her neck. "Much later."

Charlotte sighed, letting him trail kisses along her neck, collarbone, to her shoulder. She ran her fingers through his hair, keeping him close.

"Sean?" she said.

"Hmm?" he murmured, still intent on tasting the warmth of her skin.

"I don't have a home," she said. "I don't have anywhere to go."

He lifted his head. "Yes, you do. This is your home. Here, with me."

Her blue eyes searched his. "Are you sure?"

"Marry me, Charlotte," Sean said. "Marry me, live here, and never leave me again."

Charlotte's smile lit up her whole face. "I love you, Sean McKinley. And yes, I will marry you."

Sean pulled her tightly against him. It would be a long time before he let her go. But when he did, they'd spend every moment together the rest of their lives. And Sean intended to make that last as long as possible.

ABOUT HEATHER B. MOORE

Heather B. Moore is a four-time *USA Today* bestselling author. She writes historical thrillers under the pen name H.B. Moore; her latest thrillers include *The Killing Curse* and *Poetic Justice*. Under the name Heather B. Moore, she writes romance and women's fiction, her newest releases include the historical romance *Love is Come*. She's also one of the coauthors of the *USA Today* bestselling series: A Timeless Romance Anthology. Heather writes speculative fiction under the pen name Jane Redd, releases include the Solstice series and *Mistress Grim*.

For book updates, sign up for Heather's email list:
hbmoore.com/contact
Website: HBMoore.com
Facebook: Fans of H. B. Moore
Blog: MyWritersLair.blogspot.com
Instagram: @authorhbmoore
Twitter: @HeatherBMoore

Made in the USA
Middletown, DE
19 September 2018